THE GERMAN

THE GERMAN

JAMES PATRICK HUNT

FIVE STAR
A part of Gale, Cengage Learning

GALE
CENGAGE Learning®

Farmington Hills, Mich • San Francisco • New York • Waterville, Maine
Meriden, Conn • Mason, Ohio • Chicago

GALE
CENGAGE Learning®

LIBRARY OF CONGRESS CATALOGING-IN-PUBLICATION DATA

Names: Hunt, James Patrick, 1964– author.
Title: The German / James Patrick Hunt.
Description: First edition. | Waterville, Maine : Five Star Publishing, [2017]
Identifiers: LCCN 2016037337| ISBN 9781432832834 (hardcover) | ISBN 1432832832 (hardcover)
Subjects: LCSH: Intelligence officers—Fiction. | Political corruption—Fiction. | Conspiracies—Fiction. | BISAC: FICTION / Thrillers. | FICTION / Mystery & Detective / General. | GSAFD: Suspense fiction. | Mystery fiction.
Classification: LCC PS3608.U577 G47 2017 | DDC 813/.6—dc23
LC record available at https://lccn.loc.gov/2016037337

First Edition. First Printing: February 2017
Find us on Facebook– https://www.facebook.com/FiveStarCengage
Visit our website– http://www.gale.cengage.com/fivestar/
Contact Five Star™ Publishing at FiveStar@cengage.com

Printed in the United States of America
1 2 3 4 5 6 7 21 20 19 18 17

"I hate war as only a soldier who has lived it can, only as one who has seen its brutality, its futility, its stupidity."

—Dwight D. Eisenhower

"The first condition of power is the worship of power."

—Joseph Goebbels

Chapter One

On the tenth day of the thirteenth month of Miller's sentence, the assistant governor called Miller into his office and told him he would be released early for good behavior.

Thirteen months and eleven days earlier Miller had stood before a magistrate who told him: "The importing of cocaine into Britain is a serious offense. The amount of cocaine seized was sufficient to persuade this court that it was intended for sale and distribution, rather than personal use. While it is undisputed that you have no history of criminal behavior prior to this incident, this court is not in a position to ignore the facts in this instance. While you are in our country you are expected to obey our laws. I hereby sentence you to fifteen months in prison."

With that, Kurt Miller became a guest of Her Majesty and was taken directly to HM Prison Glaisdale in North London, a penal institution that was built during Queen Victoria's reign. Glaisdale was a Dickensian jail, one of the dirtiest and oldest in England. None of the cells had toilets. They had slop buckets for waste that the prisoners emptied out each morning. Miller never got used to the smell.

At the time of his sentencing, he was forty-three years old. Forty-four when he stood before the assistant governor's desk. Thinner and paler. Miller wore the used prisoner's uniform he had been issued on his arrival. Blue jeans, gray socks, blue striped shirt, denim jacket, and black plastic shoes. The clothes smelled like Miller now, rather than the inmate who had previously worn them.

The assistant governor was a man of about sixty with black-rimmed glasses, like Buddy Holly's. He wore a tie beneath his navy blue jersey. His name was Ned Loyd. He asked Miller to have a seat and offered him some tea.

Loyd looked up from his paperwork and said, "I see you've formed a taste for tea."

Miller said, "One takes what is offered."

Loyd said, "Right. When you're in the nick, you have little to look forward to. So little to do. That's why you brew tea. It occupies one's time."

"Something."

Loyd said, "You seem . . . bothered."

Miller was quiet for a moment. He was reluctant to tell the assistant warden what he was feeling. Guilt. Shame. Maybe even sadness. Miller knew his feelings were not rational.

Loyd said, "Your apprehension is actually quite normal. There are men at this institution who don't want to leave. They don't admit that, of course. Who but a madman would prefer prison to freedom? But some of these men feel at home here. Like they're with family. But you're not one of them."

"Thank you. I suppose."

The assistant warden looked at him and said, "Your English is very good. Where did you learn to speak it?"

"In school. It is not unusual in Germany."

The assistant warden said, "We don't get many Germans here, that's for sure. Your papers said you were a civil servant, based in Hamburg."

Miller didn't respond.

Loyd said, "But nothing else. What is it you did for the German government?"

Miller said, "Is the answering of that question a condition of my early release?"

"No," Loyd said. "I'm just curious about you. I've been at this job for almost forty years. These are modern times, but I'm not what you'd call a contemporary man. My view remains that the purpose of prison is to punish, not to rehabilitate. I think you've been sufficiently punished. Still, I must say I don't understand you. You're not like the other men here."

"Because I'm not English?"

"Because you're not a criminal. Not a full-time one, anyway. Ninety-nine percent of these men believe they were victims. Of society or some other unfairness. You've never claimed to be a victim." The assistant warden lifted his cup of tea. "Your cell-mate seems to think you were a policeman."

"I did not tell him that."

"No, I don't suppose you did. You worked in the shop, ran your laps in the yard during your forty-five-minute shift, you never snitched, and you kept to yourself. Not that I blame you, of course. Glaisdale is not exactly loaded with the sort of coves a man should trust. Not if he's sensible."

Miller said, "Sensible men don't traffic in narcotics."

"Ah. So now you say you didn't?"

"I've said that all along."

"You said it before the bench. But not during your stay at this institution."

Miller shrugged. "What would have been the point?"

Those unfamiliar with England often assume that it is the aristocracy that strives to keep the class system in place. Not necessarily. Often the British working class is as much invested in maintaining the class system as anyone else. It is rare, even today, to find an English non-commissioned officer apologizing for his rank. It is a sort of pride that outsiders have trouble comprehending. Ned Loyd had worked for Her Majesty's Prison Service for most of his adult life and had no regrets. He had never abused a prisoner and had never taken a bribe.

Now he regarded the German. Miller was an odd sort. To Loyd, the German did not seem of the criminal class. A quiet man without the sort of inferiority/superiority complex you saw in some Germans. Miller was not a big man. He was shorter than average and slight of build. But there was a coiled strength about him. Loyd had heard the rumor that Miller had broken a big Rastafarian's hand in the yard. Some sort of judo flip followed by a twist and applied pressure as the Rasta lay on the ground. Loyd had read the medical report, confirming the Rasta's fracture. But no witnesses could be found to uphold a formal charge. True or not, none of the inmates bothered the German after that.

There was something vaguely aristocratic about Miller as well. Perhaps it was because Miller came from Hamburg, a city some said was the most English of German cities. There was little of the *Volk* about him.

Like many Englishmen of his generation, Loyd had grown up despising Germans. The Germans had bombed London. The Germans would have enslaved England if they could have. But that had all happened long before Miller was born. Loyd's father had once said to him, "The Germans of today may not be Nazis, but I'm reasonably sure they're still Germans." Which meant . . . what, exactly? That they would "rise again"? Men of Ned Loyd's time didn't have the energy to worry about such things. They worried more about British-born Muslims putting bombs on a London bus.

Unlike Loyd's father, Loyd's grandfather seemed to admire the Germans. This had always been something of a mystery to the Loyd family. Grandpa Loyd was no Nazi sympathizer and had never once been heard to say anything against the Jews. But grandpa had fought against the Germans in the First World War and said they were good and brave soldiers and he would trust them over the French any day of the week. Grandpa said most British soldiers of his generation felt the same way.

Miller said to the assistant warden, "Mr. Loyd, I suspect you may have had some influence in securing my early release." The German looked at the floor. "If that is so, please know that I am very grateful."

And here the German seemed most vulnerable. The assistant warden understood this feeling. When a man is sentenced to prison for the first time, it is the unexpected kindness that can often undo him. It was too strong a reminder of where he was and what he was up against. To survive in prison, one generally had to accept his fate.

Loyd said, "You overestimate my influence, Mr. Miller. I had nothing to do with it." He hoped the German would accept the lie. "A word of advice, though. You will be tempted to tell the other inmates about your early release. Don't."

"Why not?"

"Let's just say I'm superstitious."

The German and the Englishman parted without shaking hands.

Jack Spanner was Miller's cellmate. Spanner was a small, balding man with a pot belly. Before being sentenced, he had worked at a betting shop. When Spanner first met Miller, he said, "I want you to understand something. I am not a criminal. I am *not* a criminal. I'm a murderer."

Initially, Miller thought that Spanner was trying to intimidate him. But then he soon realized that Spanner was actually just a snob who didn't want his cellmate to think he was common. Jack Spanner had killed his wife after he found out that she had been sleeping with his best friend. Spanner never expressed regret for what he did. It seemed important to Spanner to distinguish himself from the drug dealers and the thieves.

England was a funny country, Miller thought. But then, Miller had never been imprisoned anywhere else.

At four o'clock, per the usual routine, Miller made tea for himself and Spanner. At four fifteen, per the usual schedule, the cells were locked down for the night.

Spanner sat on his steel bed with the thin mattress and the chamber pot at the foot. Miller sat at his wooden desk. Miller had not been able to run his laps after his meeting with the assistant warden. He had not had the energy. He was still feeling ashamed and very tired. He was still feeling like a failure.

He looked at Spanner sitting on his bed, sipping his tea and looking at nothing. In all the time Miller had lived with Spanner, he had never once heard him express any remorse for killing his wife. He didn't express any regret either, not even that his actions had permanently cost him his freedom. Spanner said she'd deserved it. Miller did not delude himself with a belief that he had formed a friendship with this man. There was no community of spirit between them. They simply shared a prison cell. Spanner seemed neither to like nor dislike him. Spanner was empty of such things. Miller was not afraid of Spanner. He knew Spanner had spent his murderous wrath on the one person he had claimed to love and that was it. Spanner would live out the rest of his life at Glaisdale and die here.

While Miller would go free.

Miller said, "Jack."

"Yeah."

"I'm getting out tomorrow."

"You're joking."

"No. Early release."

After a moment, Spanner said, "You were sentenced to fifteen months, eh?"

"Yeah. I had about seven weeks left."

"Well, that's good news for you." Spanner didn't seem

unhappy or happy about it. He may have seemed glad to have some interesting conversation. It was hard to tell with Spanner. He didn't show much.

Miller said, "You can have my things, if you like."

They weren't much. A radio, a tube of toothpaste, a couple of bars of fresh soap, and two pairs of clean socks.

"You're going to leave the radio?"

"Yes."

"Thanks, mate."

That was all Spanner said about it. Still, it made Miller a little less depressed.

CHAPTER TWO

Five days later Miller was drinking coffee at a café off the Col-annaden in Hamburg. On German soil for the first time in thirteen months. Hearing himself speak his own language for a change. He had not met any other Germans at Glaisdale. He was in the British prison long enough that he found he had started thinking in English. His accent gave him away though. He had been called Fritz and Nazi a couple of times, but generally had managed to avoid fights. Fighting got you put in the hole at Glaisdale where there was an unmattressed cot and no light. He'd received survival training in his profession, but he would avoid the dark holes if he could.

Hamburg was the same and he was surprised by its same-ness. The same canals, the same restaurants, the same avenues, the same port, the same canyons of glass and steel. The city he had grown up in and that had been bombed into rubble and rebuilt long before he was born. Bombed back when there were Nazis, bombed hard enough that future generations of Germans lost their appetite for wars and empire. It was all before his life had begun, but he was still German and still ran into people who felt he should apologize for it. The Hamburg he knew was the same and he wondered now why he thought it should have changed merely because he had changed. He wondered why he should feel ashamed in his own home when he hadn't done anything wrong. During his imprisonment he'd thought a long time about what he had done right and what it had cost him.

Physically he had changed. He had lost weight in prison. His hair had streaks of gray that hadn't been there before. He thought of his father's hair when his father was the age he was now. His father's hair had not been gray at that age. But then people had always told him he took more after his mother. His parents had died before he was arrested and that was one thing to be grateful about.

It was overcast but he still wore sunglasses. He was still adjusting to daylight. He got forty-five minutes a day outside during his term, but the yard outdoors was behind a massive stone wall and the air had been stale and the light severely limited. Time served at Glaisdale was like living underground. Or in a dungeon. He was out of the dungeon now, but not yet feeling free. Not yet feeling at home.

Miller looked out at the world that had been taken from him and then looked down at the newspaper that was on the table before him. The newspaper reminded him that the United States Army was approaching the first-year anniversary of its occupation of Syria. Six months had passed since the Islamic State rebels had publicly decapitated Assad. Yesterday, fifteen American Marines had been killed by a truck bomb in Aleppo, bringing the total number of confirmed American military deaths to over twelve hundred. The White House spokesman said they had not yet determined which of the half dozen known insurgent outfits was responsible but acknowledged that the Islamic State and al-Qaeda terrorists could certainly be considered. A senator for the opposing political party blamed the President for something called "negligent security," but neglected to mention that he had supported the President's request for military action last year.

"Christ," Miller said.

Miller looked up from the newspaper and saw the woman coming toward him and it took him a couple of moments to piece together that the woman was Elsa. He didn't recognize her at first. She waved to him and smiled bravely and he wanted to think he hadn't recognized her because she looked different. But she didn't look different. She had the same hairstyle, the same fashionable clothes. She just didn't belong to him anymore. No longer his cool Berlin blonde.

The telephone call coming back to him now. They had been in the early stages of a divorce before he was arrested, but she had offered to postpone the proceedings until he had finished his sentence. He had told her on the phone not to postpone it. He did not want to take advantage of her generous nature.

He stood now and received her kiss and embrace. They held each other for a long time and he knew she still didn't belong to him. But at least the anger was gone. He had given her reason to be angry with him long before his arrest. Now it was good to touch her, to smell her perfume again.

She sat at the table with him and they waded through some uncomfortable small talk as they studied each other's expressions and body language. She did not do him the unkindness of telling him how good he looked. Or how bad.

Then she asked him when he had been released.

Miller said, "Five days ago."

Elsa said, "When did you get to Germany?"

"Tuesday."

Elsa frowned. An expression of mild anger he was familiar with. And happy to see now. "That was three days ago. And you only called this morning?"

"I needed some time alone. To acclimate."

"You had plenty of time alone there."

"That was a different kind of alone. A bad kind."

She frowned again, this time in a different way. "I'm sorry."

"Don't be," he said.

"You get out of prison and your ex-wife scolds you. What

16

must you think?"

"I must think I'm happy to see you."

"*Ach.* And your brothers? Have you called them yet?"

"Not yet."

"Oh, Kurt."

"You know Hans and I have never been close. And Sigi." Miller made a gesture of hopelessness about his brother's wife.

"She was always a bitch."

"And now she thinks I'm a criminal. Her distaste is finally justified."

"Well, fuck her. But what about Manfred? Have you tried to call him?"

"The one who *is* a criminal. No."

"You should try."

Miller smiled. She had never shown any warmth to Manfred. Never invited him to their home. For good reason, of course. Miller said, "You have changed your mind about Manfred?"

"No. But he is your brother. He would want to know you are okay."

"Maybe," Miller said. He wanted to believe it, but didn't.

Elsa said, "I'm going to have a cigarette. Do you want one?"

"Not now."

Elsa said, "I believed you were innocent. I always did. That's why I offered to stay the proceedings."

"And if you'd thought I'd been guilty?"

"Oh, I don't know. Maybe I would have still offered."

Miller smiled. "And maybe not. You believe in my innocence. But do you really know?"

"I know it because I believe it. Should there be something more? Or do you want me to write it down and sign it?"

"No. I'm grateful to you."

"As a friend?"

"As a friend."

"I think I could have been a better wife to you. We married so quickly, you and I. Too much in love, maybe."

"But not so compatible," Miller said. "But you were better at being married than I was."

"If prison has made you sentimental, I'm going to leave right now."

"It hasn't done that," Miller said. "I assure you. Are you seeing someone now?"

Elsa studied him for a moment. She had seen a hardness in his expression then that worried her, maybe even frightened her. Not when he asked her if she was seeing someone—that was an attempt to deflect the tone away from his anger. It was when he said, "I assure you." She decided it had passed.

"Yes," she said. "A lawyer. His name is Heinrich."

"Ah. Perhaps I could have used him in London."

"He doesn't do criminal work. He's an international lawyer."

"Solid choice. You like the fellow?"

"He doesn't have your style. But he's a steady man. And he's kind." She lowered the cigarette. "Kurt. He's been offered a job at the European Commission. A good job. It would mean moving to Brussels."

"For both of you?"

"Yes. He can get me a job too."

"Are you seeking my blessing?"

She laughed. "You really are a shit. I'm trying to be nice to you."

"Let me down gently, huh?"

"Something like that. Or I'm just flattering myself."

"You're not flattering yourself. Do you see yourself happy with this man?"

"I think so. One never really knows, do they?"

"No. But if your gut tells you it feels right . . ."

"It feels right." She paused and then smiled at him. "You

never liked Brussels, did you?"

"There's nothing to do there."

She laughed again. "Do you remember that time we went to that awful American restaurant in Brussels and you got so ill? You asked the waiter what he had brought you and he said, 'Some kind of beef.' "

"I think he may have been a terrorist."

Still laughing, she said, "And then we had to pull the car over before we got back to the hotel so you could open the door to vomit all over the street. My strong, brave soldier."

"Yes," Miller said, "I'm sure you will be quite happy in Brussels."

Elsa smiled for a moment and then her expression changed.

"Kurt, what will you do now? The BND, will they take you back?"

"Of course not."

"But your pension? You have almost twenty years."

"I am a convicted felon. The pension was denied."

"But if you appealed . . ."

"It has been appealed. The pension is denied. It's gone." Miller leaned closer to her and took her hand.

"Don't cry, my darling. It is not for you to cry about."

Elsa pulled her hand away. "That is a hell of a thing to say to me. You think I don't care? You think I'm indifferent?"

"No, my dear."

"You speak as if I never loved you."

"I don't think that."

"Heinrich is connected. Perhaps he could do something."

"He can't," Miller said. "Please don't ask him to."

"But—"

"Please."

Elsa shook her head and smiled at him in a different way. "You always were a bullheaded Prussian. So determined. When you've made up your mind, it is final, uh?" It wasn't clear if she was angry at him or proud. Even now he couldn't completely read her.

Miller said, "I don't want him involved. Or you. Please understand that."

"I will." She sighed and said, "I still have your clothes. And your car."

"You didn't sell the car? But it was granted to you in the decree."

"I'm not a monster, Kurt. I know how much you love that car." She gave him back her hand.

"Come," she said.

She had kept the car in the parking garage beneath their apartment. It was a brown 1979 Mercedes Benz 450 SEL with the 6.9-liter engine. Miller looked underneath it and was glad to see only a few drips of fluid on the ground.

Elsa said, "I took it out once a month. You always told me cars were meant to be driven."

"Yes. These tires, they are new?"

She nodded. "Last week. I thought you wouldn't be back for another three months."

"That was very kind of you, Elsa." Though Miller wondered if she'd gotten the tires at the same time she had decided to move to Brussels with her lover so that she would feel better. He pushed the unpleasant thought aside and told himself it really wasn't his business.

She handed him the keys and they took the elevator up to the apartment. They were in the apartment for only a couple of minutes when Miller realized she wasn't really living there anymore. It was still furnished, but it smelled empty and unoccupied. She was living with her attorney now and that had been her decision.

She showed him his clothes in the bedroom and Miller felt a sudden rush of pain. Again, it was the unexpected kindness that could undo the condemned man. Miller turned away from her, humiliated.

And felt her hand on his shoulder. She turned him around and put her arms around him.

Elsa looked into his eyes and said, "I know it's been at least a year for you. And even before that, it had been too long."

"That was my fault."

"Yes, it fucking was. But that's in the past. What we do now . . . I'm not trying to patronize you, Kurt. I want to."

"I believe you. But . . ."

"But what? You're not attracted to me anymore? Or do you think it would be too confusing?"

"Confusing," he said, like he was trying to figure it out. "No, I . . . Elsa, I don't think I can. It . . . the confinement . . . it does something to you."

For him, being inside took away his lust for women. He hadn't even looked at any pornography. It was true what they said about such deprivation. You start out thinking you'll miss sex. Later you realize you obsess far more about the absence of decent food and fresh air.

Elsa did not seem hurt. She only seemed more worried about him. She said, "I would tell you to let me know when you're ready. But I suspect you're not going to stay in Hamburg very long."

"Did I say that?" His voice a little sharper now.

"You didn't have to," Elsa said.

Elsa left him alone in the bedroom. Miller packed a few items of clothing into a suitcase. He kissed her on the cheek before he took the elevator down to the Mercedes. The car—which he had once been so attached to—did not give him much comfort. He didn't have the heart to tell Elsa he would have to sell it.

21

CHAPTER THREE

Manfred looked at the engine of the Mercedes.

He said, "I see you have replaced the hoses. And the oil filter. So much care and devotion. And yet you want to sell it?"

Miller said, "I told you. I need the money."

"But you don't ask me for a job."

Miller sighed. He was not sure if his brother was serious. Manfred often tried to be funny. It was Manfred's smile that people feared. Though Kurt had never feared him.

They were in the St. Pauli district of Hamburg. In a parking lot behind one of Manfred's sex shops. One of Manfred's girls came out of the back and showed Manfred something on an iPad. Manfred looked at the screen and told her the price was acceptable. The girl went back inside.

Manfred Miller looked at his younger brother and said, "You like her?"

"She's attractive," Miller said.

"Have you had a woman since you got out?"

"I don't need one."

"Ah. Always so Spartan, my little brother. But you could use the adjustment."

"I don't want to work for you, Manfred."

"Because you look down on me, huh?"

"I don't look down on you."

Manfred Miller ran one of the most profitable brothels in Hamburg. It was legal. He was known to have dealt in the drug trade as well. But he said that was all in the past. He had been saying that for ten years. Kurt never believed him.

Scotland Yard had questioned Kurt Miller about his brother after his arrest. They had told him that they knew he had been transporting cocaine for his brother and that he could make it a lot easier for himself if he just admitted it. Miller told them he couldn't tell them what wasn't true.

Manfred shut the hood of the Mercedes and said, "I tried to contact you while you were in London. Before you were sentenced. I could have connected you with a very good lawyer. Why didn't you take my call?"

Miller said, "It wasn't your problem."

"But I know they tried to get you to give evidence against me."

"What difference does it make now?"

"It makes a difference to me. I know I didn't give you any coke. If I had, I would have advised you to never keep it in the same car you were driving."

"It was nothing to do with you."

"You say. But perhaps you were guilty by association."

"We haven't associated in years," Miller said.

Manfred said, "That was your decision. I have two brothers. A doctor and a policeman. And it was you who went to prison." Manfred looked at Kurt. "I take no pleasure in it."

"Neither did I," Miller said.

Manfred shrugged his shoulders, giving up. He said, "Well, let's see how it drives."

Manfred had never been much of a car buff. He owned about half a dozen cars, none of them more than a couple of years old. He drove the old Mercedes without enthusiasm or interest. He seemed disappointed that it didn't have a SAT/NAV.

Manfred drove the car to a soccer field in the suburbs where young men were practicing. The coach of the team saw them get out of the Mercedes and walked over to them. Manfred introduced the coach to Kurt. That was when Kurt found out that Manfred owned the team. Manfred and the coach talked about what Klinsmann was doing for the American football team. The coach reminded them that America had twice reached the Round of Sixteen without Klinsmann, but nobody seemed to remember that. The coach returned to his work and the Miller brothers took a seat on a bench.

Miller said, "How are your children?"

"They are good. Helmut is at university now."

"What is he studying?"

"Engineering. I think he is more like you than me. Loves motors. He built a robot last year. You would have made a good engineer."

Miller shrugged. Then he said, "He knows what happened to me, then?"

"Yes. But I didn't tell him. His mother . . . I'm sorry for that."

"It's all right," Miller said. "He would have found out sooner or later."

"The irony is," Manfred said. "He doesn't really know about me. Oh, he hears things. Children talk. But he thinks I'm just a club owner. He is loyal to me. The things I've done, I suppose I would have deserved a son who joined up with the Red Army Faction. But I've been fortunate." Manfred laughed. "So far. Monica, on the other hand . . . she is a wild one. I may get my comeuppance with her."

"I hope not," Miller said. Though he had never really liked Monica. She had always been an unpleasant girl. As a young teenager, she was given to harsh declarations like "Democracy is a *joke!*" Miller didn't believe that Monica's nasty demeanor was any fault of his brother's, though. Or his brother's wife. Manfred had always been a devoted father. And despite working in the sex trade, Manfred had never been unfaithful in his marriage.

When they were children, their parents had rather specific plans for them. Hans, the oldest and, from the parents' point of view, the smartest, would be a doctor. Manfred, the affable clown, would be a baker. And Kurt, the quiet and orderly one, would be a soldier. Manfred's apprenticeship as a baker lasted only a couple of months. Kurt thought Manfred may have started selling marijuana as early as his teenage years. A few years later, Manfred was selling black-market goods he received through his contacts with American soldiers. He was a natural-born salesman and networker, the sort who could size up a man within a couple of minutes of meeting him. It annoyed Kurt because he believed Manfred would have been a big success even if he had done everything legally. But then Kurt knew part of what fueled Manfred's ambition was the desire to be a contemporary pirate. A rogue working outside the system. Manfred's easy manner hid a ruthless nature. He was not above using bodyguards to rough up people he believed were a threat to him. Though, to Kurt's knowledge, Manfred had never been involved in killing anyone.

Now Manfred said, "We haven't spoken in over a year now. So I want to ask you something."

"All right," Miller said.

"Never mind what the police think, do you think I had something to do with the cocaine being placed in your car in London?"

"I have never thought that."

Manfred said, "But you knew I was angry with you. Not coming to family events I invited you to. You knew I was angry at you for that."

"I knew. But I know you wouldn't put me in jail. I want to ask you something now. Do you think the narcotics belonged to me? Or that I was transporting them for someone else?"

Manfred said, "I don't know. It doesn't matter now."

"I'll tell you anyway and I don't really care if you believe me," Miller said. "They did not belong to me. And I wasn't carrying them for someone else."

"Then what?" Manfred said. "You were framed?"

"Yes."

Manfred took his eyes off the team sweeper who had just tried to kick a goal but went wide of the net.

Manfred said, "By who?"

"I don't know yet," Miller said. "But I will."

CHAPTER FOUR

Bruno said, "Do you remember that Ami we worked with in Mogadishu? The tall fellow who said he was from Florida?"

Miller said, "The helicopter pilot?"

"Yes."

They were at Bruno Barzen's house in Berlin. Sitting in the study sipping sherry. There was one tea cake left on the table. Bruno had eaten the rest.

Miller said, "I remember him. His name was Herndon, right?"

"Yes, that's right. Cal Herndon. God, that man just couldn't stop talking about Rommel. What a great and noble soldier Rommel was." Bruno shook his head. "He told me things about the Desert Fox I didn't know."

Miller smiled. "A lot of American soldiers admire Rommel. He's their favorite Nazi."

Bruno said, "My grandpapa said he was very brave, but a show-off and a glory boy. Most of the Prussian corps hated him for kissing Hitler's ass and look what that got him. Poor Cal. He thought he was ingratiating himself with us, idolizing Rommel."

"The Americans like to be liked," Miller said. "But Herndon was a good soldier. I don't think he was feigning his admiration for Rommel. He just preferred the Rommel myth to the reality. I tried to tell him once that Rommel was actually *not* part of the plot to kill Hitler, that he was actually loyal to Hitler until the end. But he didn't want to hear that."

"Yes," Bruno said. "It's too bad he was killed."

"Rommel?"

"No, not Rommel, you ass. Herndon."

"Herndon's dead?"

"Yes. His helicopter was shot down in Afghanistan last week. I saw it on the news."

"Christ," Miller said. After a moment he said, "Had you kept in touch with him?"

"No. Like I said, it was on the news."

"Shit, that's terrible. He was a good man."

Miller remembered what Herndon had done in Somalia. The cocky and courageous American with his cap that said "Gators" on it, buzzing through Mogadishu in an AH-6 "Little Bird," dropping it down on the ground in murderous crossfire to pick up American soldiers who were pinned down and needed to be rescued. Not for the first time, Miller thought that American soldiers were better than the people who sent them out to such places. Cal Herndon had survived that battle when men around him had been picked off by snipers like ducks at a carnival. Maybe that experience had left Herndon with the false impression that he was immortal, a delusion that Rommel himself suffered from. What was Cal Herndon doing in Afghanistan when he was already living on life's overdraft?

Miller had taken the night train to Berlin to meet with Bruno Barzen, a soldier he had served with and had worked with at the BND, Germany's foreign intelligence service. In their younger days, they had been part of Germany's elite GSG-9 anti-terrorist squad. Now they sat in front of a fire in Bruno's study at his suburban Berlin home, two middle-aged men who had grown weary of war and become pacifist in the way many soldiers do.

Miller said, "Stupid. Why are the Americans still in Afghanistan? Bin Laden is dead and buried. And the Afghans are never going to have anything like a western democracy. What is the point?"

Bruno shrugged. "Who knows? We can lecture them about the follies of empire, but who would listen to a German about such things? And Kurt, it is not as if we don't bear some responsibility in the matter. The BND promoted the invasion of Iraq and Afghanistan."

"I didn't."

"Nor did I," Bruno said. "But we don't run the BND. Men like us don't get to run things and we never will." Bruno smiled. "A good German follows orders."

"As does a bad one," Miller said. It was an old joke between them.

Bruno left his chair to stoke the fire. Without looking at Miller, he said, "I haven't asked you about your time in England. If it's not something you wish to discuss, I understand."

After a moment, Miller said, "I'm sorry for not answering your letters."

Bruno said, "You don't have to be."

"I wasn't in England on holiday," Miller said. "I was in prison. It's okay to say it."

"So you were in prison and now you're out. You don't have to explain anything to me."

"You may change your mind about that when you hear what I have to ask you."

Bruno turned to face him. "Money?"

"No, not money, you idiot." Miller said, "I need to find something out. And I need your help."

"What is it?"

"I was told that an unnamed informant telephoned Scotland Yard and told them I was transporting narcotics."

"Were you?"

Miller smiled. "Are you now asking me if I was guilty?"

29

Bruno Barzen said, "My friend, I ran up the steps of an airplane with you in Frankfurt and watched you kill two terrorists and disarm a third. We took that plane back from them and no hostages were killed. A good day for both of us. I would trust you with my life. But any man who says he knows another man completely is a liar." Bruno shrugged again. "If you were guilty, it would mean nothing to me. You would still be my brother. Every man has his weaknesses."

"Okay," Miller said. "But it means something to me. Bruno, I was innocent. Somebody framed me and I want to find out who."

"Why would someone frame you?"

"I have an idea why. But I don't want to tell you."

"Why not?"

"Because you may be questioned about it later. The less you know, the better."

Bruno sagged his heavy frame back into his chair. He took off his glasses and polished them with his sweater.

Bruno said, "I only sent three letters. I should have sent more. But I know why you didn't answer them."

"Why is that, *Herr* Doctor?"

"Because you were ashamed. No, don't look at me like that. Knowing you, you would be ashamed whether or not you were guilty. So you feel ashamed and you serve your sentence and during all that time, you think about what was done to you. Right?"

"Perhaps."

"Perhaps, Christ. Kurt, do yourself a favor. Take a holiday. Go to Spain. Go to a beach. Go get laid. It's not healthy for a man to make revenge the focus of his life."

"It's not revenge," Miller said. "It's righting a wrong. If I thought I could leave it alone and not . . . not lose my sanity, I would."

"You're the sanest man I know. No prison could break you."

"Don't be so sure," Miller said. "Will you help me?"

"You want me to find who informed on you, is that it?"

"You have contacts with MI6."

Bruno laughed. "And how would you know that? We've always worked in different sections at BND. Very few know we served together in GSG."

"You've whined about your work in your weaker moments. You're a talkative man, Bruno."

"A stupid man, if I ever said such a thing to you." Bruno began to fidget with his glasses again, but gave it up. "Yes, I have contacts. Maybe a favor or two I can call in. But don't count on me."

"I'm afraid I have to," Miller said.

CHAPTER FIVE

Manfred said, "I never liked Berlin. Too decadent."

"That speaks well of you," Miller said.

"Did you see that Wim Wenders movie?" Manfred asked. "They filmed it in Berlin when the wall was still up. These angels sitting in a BMW talking about how much they miss being on earth. And one of them says he misses the opportunity to sin. *'To lie, to be a savage, to be able, once in a while, to enthuse for evil.'* "

"I didn't see it," Miller said. "It sounds very German."

"That is not Germany," Manfred said. "Enthusing for evil—that is Berlin. Decadent, I tell you. My wife made me watch it with her."

Christ, Miller thought. His brother the pimp and drug dealer talking about decadence. And saying it while they sat in one of his sex shops. Topless girls walking around the dark and gloomy bar getting ready for the evening show. Miller found it all depressing and he wished he didn't need his brother so much.

Manfred said, "I found a buyer for your car."

"Good. How much is he willing to pay?"

"Your asking price, which was reasonable. He paid me already." Manfred walked over to the bar and went around it. Miller drifted over and took a seat. He looked at the reflection in the mirror behind the bar and saw two half-naked girls on the stage, their body language suggesting they were having some kind of argument. Then he looked at his own reflection and felt worse.

Manfred said, "Would you like a beer?"

Miller nodded. "Bass Ale, if you have it."

Manfred shook his head in mild disgust. "English. Don't you want something with some bite?"

"If you don't have it, don't worry about it."

"I have it. We get a lot of Englanders here." Manfred took a bottle out of the refrigerator under the bar, popped it open, and set it before his brother.

It was Miller's first beer since he had been released. It tasted so good he almost felt religion. Thirteen months of water and bread and tea, runny eggs and gray sausages. Thirteen months of British food and toilet paper that was hard and waxy. He'd never felt quite clean the whole time he was inside. He had gotten used to the smell of bad food and bad characters.

Manfred said, "You wanted it in American dollars, uh?"

"Yes."

"Why?" Manfred asked. "Planning a trip to the States?"

"Perhaps."

Manfred smiled. "Always so cryptic, my brother. All right, keep your secrets." Bruno poured whisky into a glass. He didn't add any ice. Manfred said, "You worked in America before, uh?"

"Briefly."

"Spying on the allies?"

Miller smiled in spite of himself and shook his head. "No. Embassy work in Washington. Security. I assure you, it was quite dull."

"Did you get to the Grand Canyon?"

"The Grand Canyon? No. That's about two thousand miles west of Washington."

"Oh, you should have gone. It's amazing, all this space."

Manfred waved his hand in the air as if to demonstrate. "You've never seen anything like it."

A stab of guilt went through Miller. He had not even known his brother had seen the Grand Canyon. Or even traveled to America.

Miller said, "When did you go?"

"Years ago with the family. The children loved it."

"I didn't know."

"Well," Manfred said, smiling. "Even gangsters take holidays."

Miller said, "Did you send Hans a postcard?"

Manfred laughed. "Of course not; he's a prick. Why would you ask such a thing?"

"I don't know," Miller said. He still felt ashamed. He didn't know why he should. He'd never felt guilty for writing Manfred off before. Manfred was a criminal, after all. But Miller was the one who had been in prison. Everything was different now. Your relationship with people changed when you needed them. Miller felt as if he could no longer afford the luxury of feeling superior.

Manfred said, "Let's get your money."

Miller followed Manfred to his office. In the hall they passed two more girls. These were clothed. The tall blonde one smiled at Miller and Miller gave her a polite nod.

Inside Manfred's office there was a man holding some sort of device that at first glance looked like a weed-eater. Then Miller realized he'd seen the device before. It was used to check rooms for electronic recording devices. A bug sweeper.

"Kurt," Manfred said, "this is Wolfgang. He used to work in a radio store before he found his real talent. I treat you well, don't I, Wolfgang?"

"Yes, Manfred."

"Find anything?"

"No, sir."

"Good. Some privacy, Wolfgang."

"Yes, sir."

After Wolfgang left, Miller asked, "How often do you have your office checked for surveillance?"

"Once a week," Manfred said. "You can never be too careful. The walls have ears. Now more so than ever, what with you federal types looking for terrorists everywhere. After the wall came down, you let the Stasi take over everything."

"That's not true," Miller said.

"It is true. After the unification, you worked with them, huh? One big happy family of Big Brothers."

Miller frowned. He had worked with former Stasi members after Germany was reunited. He had never learned to like it. He had not met one Stasi agent who ever felt any regret for what he did. They were, to a man, unrepentant. The good news was most of them were retired or dead by now.

"Yes," Manfred said, "We don't have to worry about the East Germans bugging our phones anymore. The Americans do it for them."

Manfred opened the safe and put a short stack of bills on the desk.

"Here are your American dollars. Twelve thousand of them."

"Thank you, Manfred. You did sell it, though?"

Manfred shook his head, wounded. "Of course I sold it. I have the bill of sale here. Did you think I was just being kind to you, inventing a buyer?"

"I would know you meant well."

"You would be the first," Manfred said. "Here is the bill of sale. All very legitimate."

Manfred took the papers and unfolded them. He folded them back up and put them in his jacket. "Thank you. Really."

"About a day's pay for me," Manfred said. "With your frugal

ways, you may stretch it for a few months. Longer if you work for me."

"It wouldn't work, Manfred. You know that."

"I wouldn't be giving you orders, if that's your concern."

"That's not my concern." Miller sighed and said, "I'd like to say you've done enough for a brother who hasn't been very gracious to you over the years. But the truth is, I need you to do something else for me."

Manfred's expression changed to something more serious.

"What?" he said.

Miller put a small digital recorder on the desk. It was about the size of a cigarette lighter. Manfred looked at it and said, "You want me to give you a recorded statement?"

"No," Miller said. "It's a recording of a telephone call placed to Scotland Yard. An unnamed informant telling the police that I'm transporting narcotics. He even tells them he saw me put the stuff in the car I rented."

Manfred said, "Where did you get this?"

"That's my business."

Manfred shook his head. "You got it in Berlin, didn't you? That's why you went there."

"Never mind that. I want you to listen to it."

"Why? If you know what it says already."

"I want you to tell me if you recognize the man's voice."

Manfred showed the first flash of anger Miller had seen in years. It was unusual coming from Manfred, who always seemed so unflappable and good humored. But then Miller couldn't claim to know the man his brother had become.

Manfred said, "Why would you think I would recognize this man's voice?"

"Well . . ."

"Because you think I'm still dealing in narcotics, don't you?"

Miller said, "What you do is none of my business. But I see

you have a man checking your office for bugs."

"Right," Manfred said. "Do I need to have him come back in here and check *you*?"

"Manfred—"

"Perhaps this is why they let you out early, huh? A deal you made with the police to get your brother admitting on tape that he's trafficking. Was that the deal you made?"

"It is nothing like that," Miller said. "I don't grass."

"After what I've done for you. You spend years avoiding me and then come back when you need something. I sold the car for you, didn't I?"

"Yes. If you want the money back, you can have it."

"I don't want the money back, you idiot. You are missing what I'm saying."

"I understand completely what you are saying. I can't make up for what I did in the past. I was a soldier and an officer working for foreign intelligence. I had to watch myself, watch who I associated with. I'm sorry, but that's how it was. I had to be cautious."

"You have always been cautious. Look what it's gotten you. You are a convicted felon with no job and no future."

They were both quiet for a few moments. Again Miller felt the shame of being a prisoner. And the shame of betraying his own blood. He thought of their childhood together. He had always preferred Manfred to Hans. They had fought each other and loved each other as brothers do. And they had shared a mutual dislike and distrust of Hans, a boy who had always considered himself morally and intellectually superior to them and then became even more unpleasant as he got older. Miller remembered the sadness his mother felt because her sons had drifted apart from each other. She had died hoping they would become closer. Her wish was never fulfilled because Miller held one brother in contempt for choosing to be a criminal and the other one in contempt for choosing to be a prick.

Manfred looked at his desk and said, "I'm sorry. I didn't mean that. It's just . . . my wife asks me why you never visited. My children have an uncle who never called them on their birthdays or sent them cards. You were my brother and my children grew up with an uncle who was a stranger to them. I . . . they never did anything to you, Kurt. I would have liked for them to know you."

"I know that. If I could fix it now, I would. But . . ."

Manfred made a gesture without facing him. And they were both ashamed at having let their mother down.

"Listen to me, Manfred, I need your help. I've no place else to go. I need to find out who set me up for this."

"For what purpose, Kurt? You going to kill this man?"

"No. I just want to talk to him."

"Talk to him, *ach*! Say you find him, what then? Demand his apology? Slap his face with a glove?" Manfred shook his head. "You ask me to risk my own security, my own family, so you can talk to some weasel in London."

Miller said, "There has to be a reason. Some reason this man would do this to me."

"You don't recognize the voice?"

"No."

"And yet you take it personally?"

". . . Yes. I spent more than a year in prison for something I didn't do. He doesn't know me. Why would he take part in framing me? There has to be a reason. I have to know the reason."

"I thought you were smart," Manfred said. "Smarter than me. If you were smart, you'd leave this alone."

"You were always the most intelligent one," Miller said. He didn't mean it in a nice way. It was why he had always been angry at Manfred. They had both grown up after their country had been reduced to rubble by Allied bombs and the sickness that was National Socialism. Grown up in that part of Germany that chose capitalism to communism and offered all sorts of opportunities for those who chose to work hard. Hans with his head in the books, Miller playing sports, and clever, affable Manfred always scheming and smiling his way out of trouble. Manfred had chosen to be a criminal when he was smart enough to have succeeded at being legitimate. Manfred who'd chosen wrong and stayed out of prison, while Kurt had tried to do right and had spent thirteen months shitting in a bucket.

Miller stood up.

"I'm sorry," he said. "I should have known better."

"Sit down," Manfred said.

After a moment, Miller sat down.

Manfred said, "Play the tape."

Miller played the tape. It was short and to the point. An Englishman telling a detective on the narcotics squad that Kurt Miller, a German, had brought two to three kilograms into London. The informant said that he knew Miller's brother in Hamburg was a known drug dealer. The detective tried to keep the informant on the phone for more time, but the informant said, "You have all you need," and hung up.

Miller turned off the recorder.

Manfred said, "So they tried to use you to get me."

"I think it was the other way around," Miller said. After a moment, he added, "You are not responsible."

Manfred said, "Anyone who knows you—*really* knows you—would know that you would have never carried anything for me."

"Whoever was behind this knew *something* about me. And something about you. You see, I was targeted."

"Why?"

"I have an idea why," Miller said. "But I'd rather not discuss it."

"Just as you'd rather not discuss why you plan to go to America," Manfred said. "You are free now, but you still want to stir things up." Manfred made a gesture. "All right, I leave that to you. But before we talk about the voice on the tape, tell me what you were doing in London. Was it related to your work?"

"No. I was on holiday." Miller paused, then said, "I was there to see a woman I met in Berlin. An English woman."

"Were you having an affair with her?"

"Yes."

"This woman, she was married, uh?"

"Yes."

"That's what I thought," Manfred said. "Did Elsa know about this?"

"No, I never told her. She and I were separated."

Manfred shook his head again. And Miller couldn't help but smile. Manfred was genuinely disappointed in him for committing adultery. Manfred could be funny about things like that.

Manfred said, "How do you know this woman's husband wasn't involved in this? That he didn't call the police?"

"That is not possible," Miller said. "I've met the man. He's one of these titled aristocratic Englishmen who inherited a pile and has never had a proper job. He behaves as if he's still at university. A pleasant enough fellow, but essentially an adolescent."

"And what is the status of your relationship with this woman now?"

"After I was arrested, I never heard from her again." Miller shrugged. "I guess we didn't care for each other very much. We were both bored and lonely."

"You didn't tell the police about this woman?"

"No. I didn't see the point."

"Instead, you were chivalrous and went to prison."

"It would not have made any difference."

"Let's hear the tape again."

After they listened to it a second time, Manfred said, "I don't know who this man is. If I did, I would tell you. Do you believe me?"

"Yes."

"However," Manfred said, "I know someone who used to work for Scotland Yard. A bent policeman who did some work for me. He may be able to identify this man for you."

"Christ, really?" Miller was impressed and he didn't want to be. He said, "Would he be willing to talk to me?"

"He'll have to," Manfred said. "I have too much on him."

Chapter Six

Kenny said, "Fellah I knew, he went up to Glaisdale for assaulting a police officer. His name was Jimmy Raines. You heard of him?"

Miller said he hadn't.

"Big fat fucker," Kenny said. "Drank a lot of gin. He got stopped by a copper after he piled his Jensen into a crowd waiting outside this club in Islington. By some bloody miracle of Christ he managed not to hit any of the geezers standing on the walk. They all cleared out when they saw him coming. Jimmy gets out of his car like he's just, you know, fucking parked it or something. The wheels up there on the walk, the undercarriage resting on the curb, all these club patrons staring at him like he's mad. A patrolman across the street sees the whole thing and walks over to talk to him. You know, the old 'What's all this then?' and Jimmy punched him in the gob. They gave him six months. I think he was in while you were in."

"I don't remember him," Miller said.

"You'd have remembered him. He liked to dress like a cowboy. Not that he was a poof or nothing. In fact, I don't believe he'd ever been to the States. He just liked the cowboy look. Wore this Stetson hat and boots, sauntered around like he was Randolph Scott."

Miller said, "They don't let you wear your own clothes."

Kenny stared at the German for a few moments. Then he said, "No, I don't suppose they would."

They were in a pub south of London in a village called Carshalton. It was a dingy place with yellow walls. The television showed the Match of the Day, the commentator saying that Rooney had become a true soccer mercenary, whatever that meant. Behind the bar, there was a poem on the wall that read:

Sutton for mutton,
Carshalton for beeves,
Epsom for whores,
and Ewell for thieves

Kenny Wexford was an ugly man with a bad complexion and a bad set of teeth. He was younger than Miller had expected, maybe in his early thirties. He wore a pair of skinny French jeans that clashed with his half-length leather overcoat. His face was red and veiny and it didn't take Miller long to see that he was an alcoholic.

Kenny said, "Your brother tell you I was sacked?"

"No."

"Well, I wasn't."

Miller raised a hand. "It's not my business."

"I'm going to tell you what happened."

"It's not—"

"Here's what happened: I had arrested this geezer had a Janet Street-Porter of charlie on him. Took it off him and told him I'd have a word with him later. I take it back to my flat with the full fucking intention of logging it into evidence the next day. Next day at the Old Bailey, the governor approaches me in the hall and accuses me of keeping it for me-self. I says to him: how would you know about this? Turns out the geezer has been grassing for another copper and canaried on me."

Miller said, "Janet Street-Porter?"

The ex-policeman looked at him. "I thought you spoke English."

"I do," Miller said, "but—"

"Janet Street-Porter, quarter. Quarter gram."

After a moment Miller said, "And charlie is cocaine."

"Right," Kenny said. "Don't you know nothing?"

Miller sighed and said, "Continue."

"Well my lieutenant," Kenny said, "he gives me the mince pies. Says to me, 'You've been naughty.' He's being clever, using old school Flying Squad strategy on me. Like it's all open and shut like. I tell him I was only trying to establish a contact with this bloke because I wanted to use him for an informant myself. He don't believe me, of course, the berk. He says I'm telling him pork pies. That I half-inched it for myself."

After a few moments of processing, Miller said, "He says you're lying to him and that you intended to keep the drugs for yourself."

"That's what I just told you, for fucksake," Kenny said. "Are you listening to me?"

Miller turned to look at the television and thought of Henry Higgins singing, *Why can't the English teach their children how to speak?*"

Kenny said, "Two days later, I'm being investigated for larceny. We don't even get through the interview and they tell me I can resign my post or stay on and face discipline and criminal charges. So I resigned. I mean, fuck 'em, right?"

Miller said, "What are you doing now?"

"I'm on the dole. But I've been thinking about getting in the music business. I can rap, you know."

Christ, Miller thought. This loser was sitting at a pub, knocking back Bushmills on Miller's paltry nest egg, and Miller had spent a year in prison.

Miller couldn't help asking, "How did you get to be a policeman?"

Kenny shrugged. He did not seem insulted. "I dunno. I

thought the hours would be good. And my uncle was a police-man."

There's your answer, Miller thought. He wanted to get away from this man. Miller said, "How did you meet Manfred?"

"Oh, you know. The usual business."

Miller said, "You still working for him now?"

"No, no. I offered to, mind you. But he said he would contact me if he needed me. As-needed basis and all. So here I am. What can I do for you?"

Miller said, "You worked in the narcotics squad?"

"Right."

"I'd like to play a recording for you and I want you to tell me if you recognize the man speaking."

"Why do you think I'd know him?"

"Because I think this man is one of your squad's confidential informants."

"London's a big fucking playground, mate."

"I'll give you fifty pounds to listen to the tape," Miller said. "Another two hundred if you tell me who it is."

Kenny smiled and said, "Anything for a friend of Manfred's."

Miller played the tape. Kenny listened to it and then asked the bartender to turn the sound down on the television. The football commentators went silent and Kenny asked Miller to play it again.

After the third play, Kenny said, "We did agree on two fifty, right?"

"We did."

"Right," Kenny said. "Your man's not an informant. At least he wasn't when I was working." For the first time, Kenny Wexford seemed nervous. "He's . . . er . . . something a bit more than that."

Chapter Seven

Miller said, "Tell Mr. Roth I work for Vlad."

The man at the bar said, "Who the fuck is that?"

"Vladimir Valnikov," Miller said. "He'll know who it is."

The bartender's expression changed. Miller had given him the name of probably the most prominent Russian gangster in London.

"Christ," the bartender said.

Miller stood and opened his jacket. "Relax," Miller said in Russian, then said it again in English. The bartender saw that he wasn't armed. "I come only to talk," Miller said.

The bartender left his post and came back with two big men in tailored suits. One of them was black, the other white, both tattooed. Miller saw the bulges beneath the white one's jacket. He was armed.

The black one, who went by the name Chewy, said, "State your business."

"I'm here to speak with Julian," Miller said.

"Your name, then," Chewy said.

"Sergei," Miller said, still using his Russian voice.

Jeff, the white one, said, "That's not a name I'm familiar with."

"You don't work for Valnikov," Chewy said.

"And you don't dress like a Russian," Jeff said.

"Fine," Miller said. "I'll come back later with Vlad. But he's not going to be happy about this."

"Steady on, mate," Jeff said and put one of his meaty paws on Miller's shoulder. It was a strong grip. "I'll tell him you're here and we'll see if he's available. Meantime, have a drink."

It seemed friendly enough on paper, but the man's voice was loaded with menace. And in case it wasn't clear, he said to the black guy, "Keep him here."

Jeff walked away and Chewy said to Miller, "Sit down." Another order. Miller got back on the bar stool. Miller looked at the bartender who now seemed pleased with the situation. The staff putting this stranger in his place.

Miller looked over at the black man and gave him a friendly smile. Chewy did not smile back. He only gripped the neck of his beer bottle a little tighter. Miller changed his smile and turned to face forward.

It was an upscale club, located in the St. James district, not far from the statue of Beau Brummell and the shoemakers who cobbled shoes at about fifteen hundred pounds a sole. In a moment of rare humility, Kenny Wexford had admitted he had never been in Roth's club. It was private, Kenny said. And not just private, but exclusive. For celebrities mostly, a place where Madonna and Gwyneth Paltrow went to trot out their British accents.

Jeff came back and told Miller to follow him. Miller did so and Chewy walked behind him. And during the walk, Miller tried to tell himself that Roth would think about making a telephone call to Valnikov and asking if he had a man working for him named Sergei. And if Valnikov answered no, I don't and what the fuck are you talking about, Miller could be out of luck. But then men like Julian Roth didn't want to look weak before men like Vlad Valnikov and could discover posers on their own. Hopefully that's what Roth would think and he hadn't attempted to make the call.

Miller was ushered into an office that was English modern

with a black desk and black chairs and photos on the wall of Julian Roth and British movie stars and noted soccer players. In one of the photos, a younger Julian had his arm around a rather disheveled-looking man who Miller recognized as George Best.

The present-day Julian Roth sat behind his desk. He was a handsome man in his early sixties who, like many multimillionaires, was trying to look young. Look close and you could see the roots of a hair transplant and the face that had been stretched back to his ears and cut short. He was sizing Miller up now and Miller realized he wouldn't have much time if the man had seen him before, either up close or in a photo. The bodyguards stood on either side of Miller.

Roth stayed in his chair and looked him up and down again.

Roth said, "You don't dress like a Russian."

Jeff said, "That's what I told him."

"Not every Russian is the same," Miller said.

Roth said, "What does Mr. Valnikov want with me?"

"A membership," Miller said.

"A membership?" Roth smiled. "Christ, is that all? He's welcome here anytime he likes. If he calls in advance."

"A full-time membership. Vlad doesn't like calling in advance."

"Well, I'm afraid that's out of the question. He has his own clubs. What does he want to come here for?"

"To be accepted," Miller said. "To be part of the British aristocracy." Miller smiled. "When in Rome."

The smile threw Roth. Miller could see that Roth was no fool. He saw the man's eyes narrow.

Roth said, "I've met him before at the Tramp. He seemed like a nice chap." Roth looked at Jeff and then back at Miller. "But I don't remember meeting you. What did you say your name was?"

"Sergei."

"Really?" Roth said. "What part of Russia are you from?"

"Hamburg," Miller said.

Before Roth's eyes went from narrow to wide, Miller swung his left fist into the soft part of Jeff's throat and as Jeff began to choke, Miller put his right hand into Jeff's jacket and took out Jeff's pistol and swung it into Chewy's nose. Chewy teetered and Miller kicked him square at the side of his knee. There was an awful snapping sound and Chewy went to the ground screaming and Miller smashed the pistol into Jeff's temple and he went down too.

Miller pointed the pistol at Roth and said, "Keep your hands on top of the desk."

"Oh, Christ," Roth said. "You're the German, aren't you?"

"Yes. Now keep your hands on the desk and you may get to live."

Chewy grunted and started to sit up. Miller kicked him in the face and he went back down.

"Tell your men to behave," Miller said. "Or you'll be the first one shot."

"Chewy, Jeff. Stay where you are. I'll handle this."

"No," Miller said. "I don't want them where they are. You," Miller said to Chewy. "Drag your friend over to the wall. Put your back against it and remain seated."

"I can't stand up," Chewy said.

"Crawl. Take him with you. Go on."

When they were against the wall, Miller turned back to Roth. Roth seemed to have aged a few years in the last few moments.

Miller took the digital tape recorder out of his pocket.

"Do you know what this is?"

"It's a tape recorder."

"It has your voice on it. You telephoned the police a year and a half ago and told them I was trafficking in cocaine. Do I need to play it?"

"No," Roth said. "I remember it."

Miller said, "Tell me why."

"Christ, I can't tell you why. I don't even know you."

"Right," Miller said. "We've never met before. But you made a telephone call and had me put in jail."

"Listen, I can't tell you why I did it. It was nothing to do with me."

"It was something to do with me. Why?"

"For Christ's sake, look at what you've done to my men. Look at me. I've got a bloody gun pointed at my face. You think I want this sort of bloody mess?"

"I'll kill you and them. And no one will know. Do you understand? You must tell me why."

"Look, all I did was make a bloody telephone call. I didn't plant anything on you. All I did was make a call. I'm not a criminal."

"No, you are a businessman who made a very big mistake. You want to die for a mistake?"

"Look, I'm sorry. I can give you money."

"I don't want your money," Miller said. "Now I asked you a question. Do you want to die for a mistake?"

"No."

"Then tell me why you made that call. Hurry now. You don't have much time."

Roth looked at his bodyguards and then back at Miller. A tough businessman, but most of his nerve leaving him now.

"You mustn't do this," Roth said. "You can't do this."

"Yes, I can. They'll think Valnikov was behind it. Vengeance for not letting him in your private club."

"Now wait a minute—"

"I'm going to count to three. One. Two."

"All right! All right! It was a man who came to see me. An American with proof that I'd . . . *Christ*, proof that I'd committed some sort of mail fraud. He said he would put me in jail if I didn't do this for him. He fucking had me against a wall. My family . . . everything I have . . . I couldn't go to jail."

After a moment, Miller said, "So you sent me."

"Yes. I'm sorry! Yes, I helped put an innocent man in jail. For God's sake, I didn't know you. If I'd known you, I . . . I . . ."

"You would have probably still done it."

"No. I swear on my children I wouldn't have."

"Don't bring your children into this," Miller said. "They are not responsible for your sins."

"Please don't kill me. I have money. I'll pay you to leave me alone."

"I told you, I don't want your money. I want you to tell me who this American was."

"I don't know who he was. He didn't tell me his name. . . . Actually, he said his name was Jones. Ed Jones. But it was obviously not his real name. He was some sort of government man. CIA or something, though he never said that. For Christ's sake, he showed me records. He had proof that I had committed a crime. He said he'd put me in jail if I didn't grass."

"You grass on someone who's guilty," Miller said, "not innocent."

"I had no choice. He was going to put me in jail."

"If I find out you haven't told me everything you know, I'm going to come back here."

"He was an American who called himself Jones. He said he was 'green.' I didn't know what that meant."

"Green badger?"

"I think so."

"That means he was an independent contractor," Miller said. "Someone who works for the CIA on contract only. Is that what he said?"

"That's what he inferred, yes."

51

"What did he look like?"

"He was a tall man. American with good teeth. Looked like an athlete. A Boy Scout. He was in his late forties, I'd say. He said it was my patriotic duty to put you in prison. Something about national security. For Britain and America." Julian Roth paused. "He wanted me to feel there was something noble in it, apparently."

"And did you believe that?"

"I don't know," Roth said. "The man had me, dead to rights. It didn't matter what I believed."

"Did he leave you a contact number?"

"No. He only said I had to make the call that day. No, wait, it was the next day. He said it would be my only chance. I don't know his real name. I don't know where to find him. I don't know how to reach him."

Miller saw the man's personal computer on a small table to the left of his desk.

Miller said, "Go over and sit on the floor with them. Stay there until I call for you."

Miller kept the gun on Roth as he walked over to Chewy and the unconscious man. Roth put his back against the wall and slid down to a seated position.

"Good man," Miller said. "Now put your hands on your head. Keep them there. Good."

Miller sat behind the desk. He opened the drawers but did not find a gun in any of them. Miller felt better.

It took Miller about ten minutes to find the site he was looking for. The photo of the man was not as focused as he would have liked. The man was not in the foreground. He was standing with another group of men in Afghanistan.

"All right," Miller said, motioning to Roth to come over. Miller placed Roth in the seat in front of the computer.

"Is that the man?" Miller said.

"I think so," Roth said.

"Don't tell me what you think. Tell me what you know. Is that the man who blackmailed you?"

"Yes. It's him."

"You're certain?"

"Yes. That's the man."

"Good."

Miller took Roth's cell phone and the cell phones off the bodyguards. Before he left, he smiled and said, "Guess you'll have to hire different men."

Roth said, "Seems so."

Chapter Eight

When Miller was in his early teens, a boy at school asked him if it was true that he was the grandson of Ernst Miller. Miller said he was, but didn't see what was important about it. The boy told Miller that his grandfather was a great man and a hero and asked how he could not know that.

Miller asked his father about it at dinner that evening. His father exchanged glances with his mother and told Kurt they would talk about it later.

Miller's father later told him that Ernst Miller had been a tank commander during the Second World War and was one of the top scoring aces with 172 tank kills. Ernst Miller had been famous for his ambush of the British 7th Armoured Division during the Battle of Villers-Bocage in 1944. In the space of fifteen minutes, Ernst Miller had destroyed fourteen tanks and fifteen personnel carriers. For that feat, Ernst Miller had been awarded the Iron Cross. Toward the end of the war, Ernst Miller was sent to fight the Allies in Arnhem and was killed by a Polish sniper. He died a hero of the Third Reich, even though Hitler knew it was all over by then and making heroes out of soldiers wasn't going to do much to lift German morale.

Miller's father said, "Your grandfather came from a long line of Prussian soldiers, going back centuries. It was something that was important to him, important to his identity. He was a brilliant tactician, a natural leader, and a brave man. But he was also in the *Waffen* SS, the elite unit of that time. He had joined the Nazi party. Whether out of ambition or a genuine belief in their principles, he chose to do that. I was a boy when he was killed. I can't say that I knew him or even have much memory of him. When I grew up, we were not encouraged to idolize people like Ernst."

Miller said, "Did he know? About the Jews, I mean. The extermination camps. Did he know about that?"

Miller's father shrugged. "Who knows? He didn't live long enough for me to ask him. Lots of Germans claimed they didn't know, but as a Jew once asked, 'Where did you think they were taking us? To a resort?' I'm a Catholic and I don't believe in collective guilt because it's contrary to the concept of original sin. We are each responsible for our own sins. The sin of joining in or not speaking out when we know we should. But then . . . I don't know. Part of me is glad Papa died when I was very young, because I don't know if I would have had the courage to ask him later if he 'knew.' I don't think I would have wanted to know if he knew or went along with it. He was my Papa and Mama always spoke well of him. And a man can fight courageously for an unworthy cause."

Young Kurt nodded, getting the drift, but still unaware.

His father said, "I grew up in a Germany where one feels he must apologize for being a German and men like your grandfather were partly responsible for that. I don't think you will have that problem. We are not a bad race of people. There is no such thing as a bad race of people. But the Germans like order. We're attracted to strength. Like the Russians, we are attracted to the Strong Man. And we are an insecure people. Churchill said that the Germans were always either at your feet or at your throat and though he was no saint, there was something to what he said. For all his talk, Hitler envied the British and their empire. I think he would have liked to have been accepted by them."

Miller said, "My teacher said he was a monster."

"Worse than a monster," Miller's father said. "Something more than a monster. A demon perhaps, sent from hell to wreak havoc on the world. I would love to say that I would have had no part in it had I lived in that time. But one never knows. To engage in that sort of exercise is to invite the sin of pride. And moral pride may be the worst sin of all. Most of us are equally capable of compassion and cruelty and we imperil out souls if we tell ourselves we are not capable of evil."

Young Miller said, "The medal. The Iron Cross. Do you have it?"

"I threw it away after Mama died. It meant something to her. For me, it was . . . it was not something I wanted to keep."

"All right," Miller said. He didn't know what else to say.

His father smiled. "You are disappointed, uh? That's okay. You're a boy and boys treasure such things. Soon you'll be a man and I'll have no ability to control you. And Manfred . . . well, Manfred will always do what he wants. But neither one of you will have to apologize for being Germans. It's not your sin. As for your grandfather, I would prefer that you not think of him as a hero."

"But you said he was a man of courage."

"I did. But leave it at that, uh?"

Miller didn't leave it at that, though. He respected his father by never speaking of his grandfather at school and never boasting about sharing his blood. And he remembered his father's warning not to admire Ernst Miller. But the boy named Kurt Miller could not help but entertain himself with some adolescent wishful thinking.

Such as:

What if Ernst Miller had *not* been a Nazi at heart? Had *not* been the sort of man who supported Hitler's extermination of the Jews? If that were the case, would it then be okay to tell himself that Ernst Miller had been a good man? Would it be so bad to admire his grandfather for being tough, quick, determined, and professional? A man who seemed to have been admired by both the British Army and the Germans. Would it be so bad to strive for such qualities himself? Could he incorporate the good qualities without incorporating the bad? Would his father say that it was a sin to even tempt himself with such thoughts?

In any event, for reasons that may have had to do with destiny or a genetic predisposition to carry on the Prussian tradition, Kurt Miller chose to become a soldier. And that led him to apply for a position at the GSG-9 anti-terrorist squad.

The German Army, of course, always stressed to the public that it was a "defensive" army only. As if they didn't trust themselves. And when he was a young soldier, Miller took pride in being part of GSG-9. They were the elite of his generation. They were the anti-terrorist unit the Israelis said were the best in the world. And for this, they received no medals or acclaim or photo opportunities with Hitler or any other leader. Their identities were kept secret. Miller had killed men. And he told himself that the men he killed were terrorists, not British soldiers or Russian peasants. It was different, wasn't it? Probably it was. He was to some degree the son of his father, a devout Catholic and philosophical pacifist. But he was also the descendant of a soldier of the Waffen *SS* and there was nothing he could do about that.

In his thirties, Miller mustered out of the GSG-9 unit and began working in intelligence and investigation. He found that he liked this work and that he didn't miss the rush that came with being a commando. He liked a peaceful life and he liked using his head instead of his hands.

At the BND, Miller found that he had a talent for interrogation. He developed the method used by great detectives all over the world. That is, he would put the suspects at ease, make them feel comfortable. Offer them cigarettes and coffee and simply get them to open up and talk to him. First about who they were and what they liked. And then later, about the terrorist cells they were working for and what they were planning. He had never tortured anyone or even threatened to kill anyone.

Until he'd come to London and threatened to kill the man who had made a telephone call and put him in jail. Threatened to kill an Englishman who was not in a uniform and not in a tank on a battlefield.

Why?

Because the man had taken his freedom away from him, his career, his pension, and his future. Had taken part in what the Germans called *berufsverbot*—the systematic destruction of a man's livelihood. But the Englishman had only been part of it. It didn't begin or end with the Englishman. The Englishman was part of a scheme to frame him and take him out of circulation. To discredit him. And now Miller had gotten the confirmation of something he had suspected all the time he had been in prison.

The man on the computer screen Miller had shown to the Englishman was an American named Carl Tanner. Tanner never told Miller he was with the CIA, but he had implied that he was. Miller had met with Tanner only once. That was in Berlin. Tanner was with a suit from the American State Department named Bill Carson. Tanner and Carson had asked Miller to amend a report he had written and Miller had refused to do so.

Miller had written his report after spending several days interviewing a Syrian named Ahmed Rashid. The American intelligence community had code-named Rashid "Eightball." Rashid claimed to be a chemical engineer who had witnessed the Syrian government using chemical weapons on its own people. Miller came to the conclusion that Rashid was lying about these allegations and put that conclusion in his report. Miller's superiors did not attempt to persuade Miller to change his report, but did ask that he meet with the Americans and hear their side of it.

Miller had worked with American soldiers before in Somalia and he had generally got along with them. But he had an almost instant dislike for Tanner and Carson. Carson was a man of about forty who wore expensive spectacles and a blue suit and made a point of telling Miller he had attended Harvard Law. Class of '96, as if that was supposed to mean something. Tanner was a hard-looking man with steel-gray eyes and only smiled when he seemed to be up to something bad.

It was Carson who started in on him first, speaking to Miller as if he were on a witness stand.

Carson said, "It seems to us that you haven't really tried to be fair to Eightball."

Miller sighed and said, "Let us call him by the name he gave us, Rashid. This meeting is supposed to be classified."

"Yes," Carson said. "But Eight—Rashid—is a man of great importance. He's trying to do something for his country. And you've dismissed him as if he were some sort of hustler."

"He is a hustler," Miller said. "In fact, I doubt Rashid is his real name. And I further doubt that he's a chemical engineer."

"Why is that?"

"I studied engineering at university," Miller said. "I asked him some basic questions about thermodynamics and heat transfer and I don't think he really understood what I was talking about. Even if he had studied engineering, he certainly did not graduate first in his class, as he represented to us."

Carson said, "So he wasn't an A student. That means we should discard everything he said?"

"He lied about his background," Miller said. "When they start off lying, you have to be skeptical of everything else."

"But this is not a man who's applying for a professional engineer's certification," Carson said. "This is a man who has given us evidence that Assad used chemical weapons against Syrian rebels. That's a violation of international law. This is a very serious matter."

"I take it as seriously as you do," Miller said. "That's why I spent eight days interviewing him."

"You say he's not a qualified engineer," Carson said. "Okay, that's your opinion."

"It's not an opinion. And I don't want to leave the impression that he only lied about his background. Rashid said that the Syrian Army used Sarin gas in the attack in Damascus. But fifteen soldiers in the Syrian Army died in that attack. When I asked him why the Syrian government would want to use chemical weapons on its own troops, he didn't have an answer."

Carson said, "You mean he didn't have one that satisfied you?"

"No, he didn't have one at all."

Carson sighed, demonstrating impatience before some imaginary jury. "You say he's not a qualified engineer. What then do you think he is?"

"I think he's, as you said, a hustler. I think he knows that some people in the Western powers want justification to declare war against Syria. Or justification to arm the Syrian rebels. So he tells those powers what they want to hear so he can get a green card and stay in Germany."

"That's a lot of supposition on your part."

"No," Miller said, "the man has a girlfriend in Berlin. A German girl. He wants to be with her. In fact, it occurred to me that he might even be an agent for the Islamic State, sent to us to plant false information so they could get assistance from the Western powers to overthrow Assad. They're certainly crafty enough to try that. But that's just a suspicion on my part.

Whatever his motives may be, the man is simply not a credible or reliable witness."

"You have something against Arabs dating your women?"

"Oh Christ," Miller said. "Are you really going to resort to that sort of thing?"

It put Carson back a bit, the German speaking to him in that tone. Miller saw Tanner smile for the first time.

Carson said, "Have I upset you in some way?"

"No," Miller said, resisting the urge to tell the punk not to flatter himself. "Continue."

Tanner smiled again.

Carson said, "French intelligence has concluded that the Syrian government used Sarin on the rebels. Am I to understand that they're wrong and you're right?"

"I don't know what source the French are relying on for that finding. If it's Rashid, yes, they are mistaken."

Tanner spoke then. "What is your belief?"

Miller regarded the American. "About what?"

Tanner said, "Do you think the Syrian government used Sarin on the rebels?"

"I think anything is possible," Miller said. "But I have not yet seen the evidence that the Syrian government did so. I think it is equally possible the rebels themselves used Sarin."

Tanner laughed. "On themselves?"

"Sure," Miller said. "Some of the rebels are al-Qaeda members. A good many are Islamic State. They want arms from your government and perhaps mine. Weapons to overthrow Assad. They would not hesitate to use Sarin gas and blame it on Assad to get those arms."

Carson said, "So you agree with Putin then?"

"I don't really care what Putin says. My investigation is my own. For what it's worth, the United Nations investigators are also skeptical."

"Well, we don't put much stock in what they say," Tanner said. "Maybe you shouldn't either."

"As I said before, my investigation is my own. I was asked to conduct an investigation, to interview a subject. I did so and those are my conclusions."

Carson said, "I understand that. But perhaps you allowed your own bias to influence that report."

Miller rubbed the bridge of his nose with his fingers. It was something he did when he was irritated.

"What bias would that be?"

"Maybe an anti-American bias."

Miller said, "Rashid is not an American. So even if I had some sort of problem with American policy, that would hardly enter in to it."

Tanner said, "Maybe you have some sort of problem with us then?"

Miller looked at him again. "I don't even know you."

Tanner looked back at him and said, "You don't remember, do you?"

Miller studied the American for a few moments. Then he said, "You were in Afghanistan?"

"Now you remember."

"Vaguely."

"I was there to deliver a suitcase of money to one of the Afghan sheiks. Though they say you can't buy an Afghan's loyalty, you can only rent it. What were you doing there?"

Miller realized he was supposed to be impressed. The American secret agent carrying a suitcase stuffed with hundred-dollar bills. Miller responded with a shrug. "I was sent there briefly. It was a long time ago."

"Didn't stay long, huh?" Tanner said. He smiled again, the suggestion being that Miller didn't have the stomach for it. It had no effect on Miller though.

"I don't think any of us should have stayed there long."

Carson pounced on that. "So you don't think the United States should still be in Afghanistan?"

"I don't think most Americans think you should still be there. That's what your polls say. But it makes no difference to me."

Carson said, "So we should just leave Afghanistan to the Taliban and Syria to that butcher, Assad? We should just let the people of those countries suffer?"

"Mr. Carson, what you do is up to you. We're just talking about a report, aren't we?"

Carson said, "Look, Turkey, Saudi Arabia, the French . . . they're all lined up on this thing. I just don't understand why you can't get on the same page."

"If you have all those nations on your page, then my report should be of no hindrance to you. I will say that if you think getting rid of Assad is going to help you, you're badly mistaken. Those rebels you seem to put so much stock in are the same sort of people who brought down the towers in New York. My own feeling is that you should leave the bees in the hive. Assad may be brutal, but he's no Islamic fanatic."

"He's violated international law."

"Not according to the United Nations," Miller said. "Listen, gentlemen, I'm no policymaker. I'm just an investigator and intelligence analyst. But any sensible man can tell you that if you proceed with this, you're going to empower your enemies."

"Not all of the rebels are al-Qaeda or members of what you call the Islamic State," Carson said. "Some of them are moderate."

"Well good luck sorting them out," Miller said.

Tanner said, "We had hoped you could be reasonable about this. But you don't seem to want to do that."

"If by being reasonable you mean I should amend my report, then I'm afraid I can't help you."

"And what if we go to your superiors?" Tanner said. "What then?"

"Do what you like," Miller said. "But I'm not going to change it."

Tanner turned to the suit and said, "Let's go. We're wasting our time with this guy."

Tanner stood and said to Miller, "This isn't over."

Miller realized then that he was being threatened. Normally, he would have let such a thing pass, but he just couldn't make himself sit quietly in that moment.

Miller said, "Mr. Tanner, you choose to flatter yourself by thinking I have some sort of dispute with you. I have no opinion of you one way or another. If you're determined to have your war, go ahead with your plans. It's your country and your soldiers that will pay the price for it. But you're on German soil now and in no position to make demands on me."

Miller remained seated. He could see that Tanner was thinking of hitting him. It would be the first physical altercation Miller would have in years. But Miller was ready to defend himself, more than ready to inflict pain, and Tanner knew it.

Tanner sensed something then. Some quality about this somewhat undersized German that had led the men in Miller's GSG-9 squad to call him their *vielfray*. Wolverine being the English translation. Vicious, quick, and able to kill prey many times its size.

The moment passed. Tanner laughed and said, "Tough guy, huh? Well, we'll see."

Then he walked out, the suit named Bill Carson walking out after him.

Two days after that, another American from the Defense Intelligence Agency (DIA) came to see Miller. He was another handsome man with American football player looks, but he was polite and seemed generally interested in what Miller had to say. The DIA agent's name was Paul Posner.

Miller was wary of him at first, believing that Posner was the good cop follow-up to Carson and Tanner's bad cops. He waited for Posner to try to cajole him into changing his mind about his report. But Posner didn't do that. Rather, Posner seemed genuinely interested in how Miller reached his conclusions. Something else, he seemed more than interested in what Tanner and Carson had said to him. Miller told him they had not been pleased with his findings.

Eventually, Miller said, "Why don't you ask them about it?"

The American named Posner seemed uncomfortable with the question. After a moment, Posner said, "Those guys are with the State Department. I work for the Department of Defense."

"But don't you all answer to the same President?"

"You would think," Posner said and then seemed to regret saying it.

"Excuse me?"

"Nothing," Posner said. "Getting back to your report, you think Eightball is a fraud?"

"Yes, I do."

"Your superiors seem to think pretty highly of you."

Miller shrugged.

Posner said, "I think State wished you hadn't written that report."

"They made that rather clear."

"Well, it's done," Posner said. It was difficult to see whether or not Posner was pleased about it. "I'm not sure what we're going to do about it."

Miller said, "What you do with it is up to you. But I trust you are going to forward it to your people?"

"Oh, of course," Posner said.

Miller wanted to believe the man. But he told himself it was out of his hands.

Two weeks later, Miller was arrested in London.

Three weeks after that, the United States and France began dropping bombs on Syria. A few months after that, the rebels executed Assad. The American President promised the American people that ground troops would not be sent into Syria. But two months after his speech, a U.S. Navy jet was shot down outside of Aleppo. The pilot parachuted to the ground and was captured by Islamic State rebels. They decapitated the pilot and then released a graphic videotape of it to the public. That led to the passing of a congressional resolution authorizing the use of all "reasonable and necessary" force. (The language of the resolution did not contain the word "war.") American tanks soon rolled into Syria, followed by American infantry. There was no welcome for the liberators this time. The Americans couldn't differentiate the friendlies from the enemy or enemy sympathizers and even those who were initially grateful for their presence began to resent the foreign occupiers, which history had always shown to be the case. Teddy bears and other stuffed animals began to be placed on the lawns and steps of family homes of the American soldiers who were killed in Syria. Permanently maimed servicemen received standing ovations at the President's State of the Union address, with members of both political parties clapping away their own culpability. Moments of silence observing the sacrifices of the men and women of the American armed forces became a regular part of the beginning of college football games. Citizens cheered when military jets roared a low V-formation over the stadium before kickoff at the Super Bowl.

To Miller, sitting in a British prison, it all seemed vaguely German.

★ ★ ★ ★ ★

Now Miller sat in a cheap hotel room in north London and put it together.

Julian Roth had identified Tanner as the man who forced him to frame Miller and send him to jail. Miller had always sensed that Tanner and Carson might have had something to do with his arrest and imprisonment. But he often dismissed the thought because he feared it might be a sign that he was losing his sanity. Literally going stir crazy. Another prisoner claiming the Establishment fucked him over. Miller simply thought he wasn't important enough to frame. He had never wanted to make his mark on the world. His only ambition had been to be a soldier. Then when he found soldiering dull and unchallenging, he sought work in intelligence and counter-terrorism so he could use his mind. He liked analyzing information. He liked interviewing witnesses and suspects. He liked summarizing his data and preparing concise, thoughtful reports. He had taken far more pride in that than he had shooting any terrorist.

But now it was clear that he wasn't paranoid. That he was not crazy. And rather than being angry about it, he almost felt relieved. Relieved to know that prison had not made him insane and self-absorbed in the way the paranoid are. Tanner had framed him. Tanner had even warned him that he was going to hurt him. *This isn't over,* Tanner had said and it wasn't idle tough talk. Tanner meant it.

Strangely, Miller almost felt an admiration for the Americans. Tanner and Carson had known that killing him would not have been the right play. If Miller were dead, his report would have still been a factor working against them. Tanner had figured out that it was better to *discredit* Miller. That he could invalidate the report by invalidating the man who wrote it. Who should rely on a report written by a convicted criminal? A report written by a drug dealer? A man whose brother was a known criminal?

Who should let such a man get in the way of going after a monster like Assad?

And they had succeeded. Miller's report was buried, Eightball was rehabilitated as an intelligence source, and the Americans got the justification they needed to drop bombs on Syria. They had gotten their war.

You're 44 years old, Miller thought. Another thirty or so years of life left if he was lucky. He could forget about this and get on with his life. He was alive, after all. When he was trained in anti-terrorism, his instructor had told him that professionals did the job and didn't take things personally. When he worked in intelligence, he treated humanely some of the most savage terrorists on earth. He had even sat in rooms with them impassively while they called him a Nazi or a pathetic tool of American imperialism. He knew there was no point in hating them, be they simply misguided or stone evil. Hating got in the way of the professional. And if he lost his humanity the terrorists would indeed "win."

So forgetting about it would be the smart thing to do. But . . . he had never claimed to be smart. Smart was something his brothers were. What he had that his brothers didn't have was a certain stubborn pride. Manfred was right. He had looked down on him. As he had looked down on his brother, who seemed to care only about money. He could forget about this and try to find a job.

But then . . . who would hire him? He was finished at BND. And he was too old now to work as a bodyguard. And even if he were younger, bodyguard work would bore him to tears. The money he had from the sale of his beloved Mercedes wouldn't last more than a few months. And the thought of going to Hans for help made him ill.

So money was a factor. But he realized that pride was probably a stronger factor. The Americans had taken away his pen-

sion, his career, and his livelihood. They had made him spend a
year defecating in a bucket. They had taken from him his present and his future. Yes, beating up the big men who worked for
Roth had made him feel better. He had enjoyed hurting them.
But they were nobody to him. They hadn't had any part in what
was done to him. They were bystanders. The real culprits were
over in America and he was but a footnote in their schemes. If
that. And if they gave him much thought at all, it was probably
to laugh over what they had done to him. They had put the
cocky little kraut in his place. They had shown him what real
power was.

And maybe there was something more to it. Or something
less. Maybe Tanner had made his decision when he tried to
physically intimidate Miller and Miller had let him know in that
moment that he would beat him senseless if it came to that.
Like boys in high school. Tanner had his chance then and he
had backed down. Had saved his anger for a better time. Maybe
it had been something as petty as that that made Tanner decide
to destroy him. People in prison killed each other for lesser
things.

This isn't over, Tanner had said.

And now Miller thought, *no, it isn't.*

CHAPTER NINE

Miller came into the United States through Canada. He carried Swiss identification identifying him as Alfred Brecht, a citizen of Berne. He had gotten the papers through a friend of Manfred's. He had not wanted to ask for Bruno's help on that matter. Bruno had done enough for him.

He bought a car at a suburban lot in upstate New York and paid for it in cash. It was a green '97 Jaguar XJ6, the last of the line before Ford bought out the company. It had a lot of miles and some tears in the driver's seat, but the compression was still good and its previous owner had taken good care of it.

He drove the car to a town in central Ohio. In the newspaper he found an advertisement for a local gun show at the county fairgrounds. He checked into a hotel and stayed the night. The next day he went to the gun show and paid fifteen dollars to get in.

It was like nothing he'd ever seen before. A massive warehouse filled with rows of tables manned by overweight middle-aged men in beards. He lingered briefly at a table where they sold Nazi artifacts. It mystified Miller. He'd never seen such things displayed as sales goods before. Uniforms of the Afrikan Corps, photos of German Tiger tanks, Luger pistols, and so forth. The salesman had a swastika tattooed on his hand. Miller wanted to lean over the table and slap the man across the face. But he didn't. An Israeli soldier Miller had once worked with had told Miller he had been to an American gun show and seen much the same thing and tried to goad the American Nazi into a fight, until his American friend pulled him away. Losers, Miller thought.

At another row, Miller accidentally bumped shoulders with a much bigger man, walking in the opposite direction. Before Miller could apologize, the big man apologized himself, earnestly in fact, and Miller said he was sorry as well, and they backed away from each other with friendly smiles. And Miller thought about what a different country America was. They both thought the other might be carrying a weapon. That was why they were both so gracious. Perhaps an armed society was a polite society.

Miller stopped at a small table with an old man sitting behind it. The man wore a U.S.S. *Ronald Reagan* hat. The man had a glass case with some pistols in it. Miller engaged him in polite conversation and the man told him he had been a paratrooper in Korea, but broke his leg falling off a ladder and was sent back to the States. The man said he had never fired a shot, but had lost a couple of good friends to the Chinese.

Miller said, "It happens."

"Good luck and bad luck," the old man said. "But we chased them out of Seoul."

Miller knew something about it. President Truman had brought his country into a war while never calling it a war, but a police action. Maybe he had been the one to set the precedent. Or maybe it had been Woodrow Wilson who had been the first to break away from George Washington's advice never to make another country's interest their interest.

"You're not a fed, are you?"

"Pardon?" Miller said.

"You're not a federal agent, are you?"

"Oh, no. Just a tourist on holiday."

"Okay. I've got nothing against Germans."

"I'm Austrian, actually."

"Oh. Like the governor of California."

Miller smiled. "Right. Like him."

"I see you have an interest in this Ruger."

"Yes. It's a nice gun."

The old man took it out of the glass case and handed it to him. "You've got a good eye, friend. This was the model that William Devane used in *Rolling Thunder*. Did you see it?"

"I'm afraid not."

"Great movie. He made 'em pay."

Miller hefted the revolver. He liked its weight and balance.

"You have rounds?" Miller asked.

"I can spare two boxes. Give you the rounds and the revolver for six hundred. Can throw in the case for another fifty."

Miller didn't need the case, but he liked the old man. He was well mannered and he didn't ask many questions. He had forged much of his identity on almost serving in a war that had been fought decades ago, but perhaps he couldn't help himself.

Miller paid him in cash. On the form he signed his name Stephen Edberg.

The waiter was a young skinny man with thin hair that fell down over his eyes. He came back while Miller was still eating and said, "Is everything still awesome?"

Miller looked up from his meal. It was the third time the waiter had checked on him in the last ten minutes.

"It's fine, thank you."

"Well, if there's anything you need, my name is Mark."

"Yes, you told me that already." Miller forced a smile. He was trying not to be rude.

"Save any room for dessert this evening? We've got a fudge brownie that is ah-mazing."

"No, thank you. Some coffee, please."

"You got it."

Miller was at a restaurant in Pennsylvania. A chain restaurant of some sort where they had a lot of distracting colorful knick-knacks on the walls. The food was not awful, but not good either. The portions large enough to feed two people, if they cared to eat it. No wonder there were so many fat people in this country. Miller wondered if the waiter was some sort of mental patient, being so ridiculously attentive and intrusive. Was there a hidden camera somewhere for *Candid Camera*? *Let's see how long it takes Mark to drive the foreigner crazy?* Wasn't it enough just to serve the food? But then Miller looked around the restaurant and realized that all the wait staff acted the same way. So they were doing what they were supposed to be doing. Smiling and chatting up the customers. Miller felt sorry for the servers. It had to be hard work, pretending to like people. He wanted to tell the waiter to quit trying so hard.

Miller remembered that American waiters were paid less than Europeans and relied more on tips to make a living. He left a twenty percent tip and left the table before the waiter could accost him again. Then he drove to a Comfort Inn and booked a room. In his non-smoking room, he watched the local news and weather and sports.

It had been a few years since he'd lived in America. Embassy duty at Washington where he had thought he might die of boredom from the work. Clinton was President then. Miller had watched the impeachment proceedings with European detachment and some bewilderment. Running Nixon out of town had made sense; there had been plenty of evidence that he had abused the powers of his office and that he was a pretty nasty piece of work, even for a politician. But Clinton had only been serviced by some poor girl who mistakenly thought he was something special. A girl he didn't even have the decency to make love to. Why impeach him for that? Maybe it had had something to do with America's puritanical roots. Schroeder, Chancellor of Germany, had been married four times and was so vain he once sued a newspaper for claiming that he dyed his hair. These things didn't particularly bother the Germans. They more or less took Schroeder for who he was. Miller believed the Americans would probably do the same for Clinton. Indeed, the bad-boy adolescence was part of his appeal. That being the case, if Clinton wanted a mistress or someone else for a wife, why didn't he just do it? Why had he lied so extensively about something so inconsequential? Why did he send his people out to trash the poor girl's reputation instead of just coming clean?

Pennsylvania and American television depressed Miller. He was out of his element. A stranger in a land he had never really felt comfortable in and, despite the couple of years he had lived there, had never fully understood. He didn't like the food. He didn't like the way cigarette smokers were treated like lepers. He didn't like food servers oppressing him with false empathy and undue familiarity. He was carrying a passport that said he was Swiss and even that small deception made him wonder if he was in danger of losing his identity. He knew he needed the false identification in the event the Americans had put him on some sort of list keeping him out of the country. It was a necessary precaution, but it still bothered him, still made him feel like he was hiding who he was because he was ashamed. But he was not Swiss or American or English. He was a German who belonged in Germany. As nice as Switzerland was, it was bland and unfeeling to him. Nothing there but banks, cuckoo clocks, and Calvinist resolve. And he would never be able to be an Englishman, for the English consider any man not born there a foreigner, even if he has lived there most of his life. He missed Hamburg, with all its damp seediness and mystic beauty. He could go home now and forget about this mission, but in a sense, it wasn't his home anymore. Until this thing was figured out, until he made some attempt to at least . . . *resolve* it, he would not feel at home in Germany. He had a vague fear that being idle in Germany might destroy him.

He really didn't even know anyone in this country. No one he could call a friend. The men he had worked guard duty with at the embassy had all gone back to Europe. It had been so long ago. A different country, really.

He knew someone though. Someone he had talked to the day he met Tanner and Carson. That man had seemed decent and unsure of what his country was getting into. He would have to talk to that man and find out what it was that was bothering him. It would be a start.

Two days later, he knocked on a door in Chevy Chase, Maryland. An attractive woman of about forty answered the door. She wore a green skirt and a green top. She seemed tired.

Miller said, "Is this the Posner residence?"

"It is," the woman said. She seemed wary of him, understandably. Only salesmen or political candidates running for city council knocked on doors anymore.

"My name is Kurt Miller. I came to see your husband."

The woman shifted her weight and looked at him again.

"How do you know my husband?"

"I worked with him in Germany. Last year."

"When last year?"

"It was about fourteen months ago. He was in Berlin. I work . . . I worked for the German government at the time."

The woman looked back at him and said, "My husband's dead, Mr. Miller. He was killed at a liquor store in Arlington last year."

CHAPTER TEN

She told him she had to leave for a spin class in twenty minutes, but if he wanted to come in for a quick cup of coffee, he was welcome. Miller wasn't sure the offer was sincere, but he accepted it anyway.

It was a nice house with a clean kitchen with expensive pots and pans hung by the sink. A design Miller suspected had come from a magazine or perhaps from watching a movie. It felt more like a display than functional. Miller wondered if she was trying to seek comfort in order and nice things. There were no photos of Paul Posner in the kitchen.

She made the coffee in a Krupp coffeepot. Krupp being the German company that used to make weapons for Kaiser Wilhelm and Hitler. Miller sat at the kitchen table.

The widow Posner brought him a cup of coffee on a saucer and asked him if would like some milk. Miller said he would. She brought the milk back to him, but did not sit down with him.

An attractive woman looking at him now, wondering why she had let him in. He seemed harmless enough to her. Well mannered and clean.

She said, "Listen, my husband never said anything about you."

Miller said, "I would not have expected him to. I imagine his work was classified. You knew he was in Germany, though."

"I knew he'd gone to Europe," she said. "He didn't speak German."

"He didn't have to," Miller said. "I speak English. Most of us do at BND."

"BND. What's that?"

"The German intelligence service."

"Well . . . I don't know."

"You are uncomfortable," Miller said. "I understand that. You don't know me. But I remember your husband. He was a good man who I think was genuinely interested in the truth, rather than serving someone's agenda. Does that sound like him?"

"He didn't talk much about his work."

"Was he still working for the Defense Department when . . . when he died?"

"No, he had resigned. He was going to work for a contractor in Virginia. He said he'd had enough of public service."

"He told you that?"

"Yes."

"Did he tell you why he'd had enough?"

"No."

Miller put his hands around the coffee cup. "Weren't you curious?"

The woman sighed and sat down at the table. "Let me tell you something. When Paul proposed to me, he said he only had one condition and that was that I never complain about his work or ask him to find a job that didn't involve so much travel. He was upfront with me and I agreed to his condition. So we married and when he was in town, he was usually home by eight o'clock. That arrangement was okay with me. I never asked him to quit. It was his decision. When he quit the job at Defense, he told me that it was because he wanted to spend more time with me and I chose to believe him."

"And now?"

The woman gave him an unpleasant look. "What does that mean?"

"I just want to know if you believed him."

"I told you I did," she said. "What are you up to, anyway? Are you a reporter? One of those truthers?"

"What is a truther?"

"It's—God, you don't *know*?"

"No."

"A truther. One of those conspiracy nuts who says the Israelis or the CIA was behind the terrorist attacks on 9/11. I really don't need that right now."

"No, I am not a truther. Not as you define it. Tell me what happened to your husband. Please."

"He dropped by the liquor store about a mile from here to buy me a bottle of wine. It wasn't for him, it was for me. He didn't drink. It upset his stomach. Anyway, he went in there to buy some wine and a man came in and held the store up. The man killed my husband and the sales clerk. There was no one else there. It was a robbery."

"In this neighborhood?"

"Is that so strange?"

"I don't know," Miller said. "It seems rather upscale for that sort of thing."

"It falls on the just and unjust alike."

"I don't understand."

"Bad luck. Tragedy. Murder. It's all random. Are you here to tell me it wasn't random? That he was targeted or something?"

"This store," Miller said. "Was it a place he went to often?"

"Yes. About twice a week, I'd say."

"So it was part of his routine?"

"I guess so."

"Perhaps it was random," Miller said. "But perhaps it wasn't. Perhaps he was followed by someone who wanted to know where he would be and when. Your husband knew something I don't think he wanted to know."

"So what then? The government killed him?"

The woman's cell phone rang.

"Excuse me," she said and answered the phone. She stood up and moved away from the table.

"Yes, Tony. . . . Yes, we're still on. . . . No, I thought you were going to make the reservation." Mrs. Posner forced a smile. "That's not what I remember. . . . Yes, I'll take care of it. . . . Okay. I'll see you then."

After she clicked off her phone, she went to the cabinet and poured herself a glass of wine. It seemed strange to Miller, a woman drinking when she said she was going to an exercise class. She leaned up against the kitchen counter with her drink.

She said, "That was a friend."

A boyfriend, Miller thought. But it was none of his business. It had been a year since her husband's death. She could date if she liked. Still . . .

Miller said, "Did they find the murderer?" He was fairly certain he knew the answer already.

"No. The police told me there was a video camera in the liquor store. An old fashioned one that used a videotape. Whoever did it took the videotape afterwards."

"So the killer knew about the place."

"I didn't say that. It could have been some gangbanger or a crackhead. They would know how to do that. This is Washington, D.C., you know. There's a lot of crime here. We have all sorts of gun control, but the criminals still manage to get guns."

"Is that what the police told you?"

"They didn't have any answers. They just expressed their condolences. One of the cops suggested I sue the owner of the liquor store for negligent security."

"Did you?" Miller regretted saying it immediately.

"I looked into it," she said, "but . . . I just wanted to put it behind me."

He hadn't offended her after all. And her lack of offense bothered him.

"Why?" Miller said.

"What do you mean, *why*? I told you, I wanted to put it behind me. For God's sake, are you judging me? Look, we—we weren't happy, okay. We were talking about getting a divorce. But that doesn't mean I was relieved when he died. Who are you, anyway?"

"I was an intelligence agent for the German government. Somebody framed me for a crime I didn't commit. I had written a report that made some Americans unhappy. They wanted to discredit me, so they had me framed and put in jail. Your husband knew about this report and was concerned about it."

"And what then? The people who framed you also killed my husband? Is that what you came here to tell me?"

"I didn't come here to upset you, Mrs. Posner. But I would like to know if your husband said anything to you. If he told you that this thing was bothering him."

"He didn't tell me much of anything and he certainly didn't tell me anything about you. Look, I really don't want to get involved in this. It's in the past."

"Mrs. Posner, we're talking about your husband. If he was murdered by someone—targeted for murder—wouldn't you want to know about it?"

The widow put her wine glass on the counter.

"I think you should go now."

Miller stood up and put on his overcoat. He looked at the widow with her wine glass and work-out clothes and said, "This man you're seeing, were you involved with him before your husband was killed?"

"How dare you!"

"Just tell me."

"So what if I was? That doesn't mean anything. You talk as if I were glad he was killed."

"I don't think that," Miller said. "But it might explain your behavior."

"What behavior is that?"

"The drinking. The self-loathing."

"The only person I loathe right now is you. You're despicable for saying that."

"I spent a year in prison for something I didn't do," Miller said. "And your husband was murdered."

"It was not what I wanted."

"Did you tell the police about this lover of yours? I'll wager you didn't because you feared they might think you had something to do with his murder. You or your sweetheart. They would not have thought that, you know. They're smarter than you realize. But you didn't want to take the chance, uh? So the police tell you your husband was killed by an armed robber and you decide to accept that theory without any further inquiry. And then time passed and you asked yourself if you sold him out, but now it's too late to harass the police for more details because then they might find out more about your affair. And you don't want that, do you? You're just going to keep on torturing yourself."

She threw the wine glass at him. Miller ducked and the glass sailed over his shoulder and shattered on the kitchen table. The widow put her face into her hands and began shaking with sobs.

Before he left, Miller told her he was sorry.

Miller stopped at a diner north of Baltimore. He ordered a BLT. It came back with enough French fries to feed a family. More American portions. Miller just ate the BLT.

A television showed the nightly news. Eight U.S. Marines had been killed by a suicide bomber at a café in Damascus. One of the customers groaned and asked the waitress behind the counter to switch it to the Ravens game. Another customer said the man should show some respect for the troops. The waitress said, "Alright, al*right*" to pacify them both before she switched the channel. Miller sipped his coffee and thought about the widow.

He had interrogated women before and been tough with them. One of them had been a German girl of nineteen who had helped kidnap a judge in Cologne and had been there when the judge was shot in the head by another terrorist. The girl came from an upper-class family in Aachen and she brimmed with hate. She expressed no remorse for what she had done. The judge was a pig, she said. A tool of the American government. She believed all the things she said. Miller spent three hours with her before tricking enough information out of her to locate her terrorist boyfriend. The experience was so unpleasant it left Miller glad he had never had children.

The widow Posner was not evil. She wasn't even really bad. She was just weak and ineffectual and lost. Miller regretted the way he had treated her. She had had no part in what had been done to him. He realized now he had taken his anger out on her, even after he had gotten all the information he needed out of her. Perhaps it was because he had been shocked to learn that Paul Posner had been killed. He hardly knew Posner. Their time together had been brief, but he felt that Posner was an honorable man who'd deserved better. He could tell himself that now his mission would incorporate vengeance on Posner's behalf, but he knew he was still acting primarily for himself. Posner's wife would not want him to succeed.

A man Miller had worked for at BND once said to him, "The reason you're so good at the interrogations is that you're good at pretending to care about these people. You're a natural actor. They don't know you're cold."

His boss had meant to compliment him when he said that. And that was how Miller took it.

CHAPTER ELEVEN

The men at the bar watched a golf ball on the big-screen television, the ball rolling ever closer to the hole as the men raised their voices, anticipating it, rolling, rolling, and then it dropped in as one of the men cursed and the other whooped in delight.

The young hedge fund analyst in the tailored suit said, "You owe me ten thousand dollars."

"Shit," Bill Carson said. "Listen, I don't have my checkbook on me. Let me just buy the next round."

The hedge fund man said, "You made a bet."

Carson noticed the bartender nearby, close enough to hear them talking. She was a young, good-looking black girl. He didn't want to look cheap in front of her.

Carson said, "I'm good for it."

"Bring it to me in cash, tomorrow."

"You'll get it."

Carson succeeded in hiding his irritation. Ten grand was lunch money to the hedge-fund analyst, but to Carson it was real money. He had only been working in investment banking for a couple of months, making a lot more than he had when he worked at the State Department. But ten grand was still a lot. New York was an expensive town.

The black girl said, "Another glass of wine?"

"Sure," Carson said. "Say, what's your name?"

"Sandra."

"How long you worked here?"

She wore the smile she reserved for customers. "About ten months."

"You from New York?"

"No. Jersey."

"Oh, I am sorry."

She kept the smile.

"Just kidding," Carson said. "You got another job?"

"Yes. I work one night a week at a comedy club."

"Yeah? Which one?"

"It's downtown," she said, still smiling, but not giving him the name. The hedge fund analyst noticed the omission and grinned.

Carson didn't notice it. He said, "You need help?"

The smile weakened and then disappeared. "Excuse me?"

"Help," Carson said. "Everyone needs help."

"No," she said, "I'm doing fine. But thank you."

"Sister, you give it some thought. Here's my card. Call me when you change your mind."

She pulled the card to her end of the bar, a half-measure. Her chin quivered, knowing he'd insulted her in the way men like him could. She went to the back of the bar to get him another glass of wine.

"Christ, Bill," the hedge fund analyst said.

"What?"

"For a guy that worked in politics, you're about as subtle as a kick in the nuts."

"Oh, fuck you."

"The poor girl's just trying to make a living. You don't come into her place of work and offer to buy her."

"I was just joking," Carson said. Though he knew he hadn't been.

"She didn't think so. Seriously, don't do that again. I like

85

coming to this place."

Carson got off his stool and put some money on the bar.

"I've gotta get up early."

The hedge fund analyst said, "Don't forget what you owe me."

"Yeah," Carson said, "about that. I was only kidding when I made that bet. So fuck you very much."

After the hedge-fund analyst left, the bartender who told customers her first name was Sandra complained to the manager. The manager was unsympathetic, saying, "What do you expect? This is Manhattan. It's filled with assholes with money trying to impress people. What, you want me to throw out everyone who flirts with the help?"

"I'm not something to be bid on," the black girl said. "I wanted that, I'd work at a strip club."

"Christ, he tipped you, didn't he?"

"Three dollars on a fifty-dollar tab. Not enough for what he put me through."

"The other guy left something, didn't he?"

"Yeah."

"So what then? It all evens out."

"You're missing the point."

"This is a people-pleasing business. You're friendly to the customers, give them a smile to show that you like 'em even when they're douchebags. You know how it works. You got a prime shift, so my advice is, don't screw it up."

"I'm not a prostitute."

"Oh shit." The manager sighed again. All the melodrama he had to endure. "Who said you were? Look, you got another customer at the bar. Take care of him and we'll talk about this another time."

Sandra went to the bar where a man sat alone. The man had

The New York Times resting in front of him. Because of this, Sandra was left with the impression that he hadn't been listening to her complain. It made her feel a little better.

She said, "And how are you this evening?"

"I'm fine," the man said. "I'd like a Bass Ale, if you have it."

"I do," she said.

She spent the next hour talking with the customer. He was polite and, in an old-world sort of way, charming. Mostly, he was different from most men she met. He didn't come on to her and he put her at ease. And when he later asked her to help him, it didn't take her long to agree to do it.

When Carson got the call inviting him to the hotel room, he was surprised more than intrigued. It brightened his mood. He'd never been with a black girl before. There had been whores, but they were mostly Asian. When the black girl called him, he was actually reluctant. Not because he doubted her interest in him. He was a player, after all. A man who was likely going to be working in the White House after Lindsey got elected. But it was late when she called and he was tired and ready for bed.

But she insisted that they meet tonight. She said she really thought he was someone she wanted to get to know.

Carson asked for the hotel room number again, asked for the address, and she said, "Great. I'm really looking forward to it."

"Me too," Carson said.

He had taken his tie off when he got back to his apartment. He thought about putting it back on, but then caught sight of himself in the mirror. No. He looked good without the tie. Dark suit and a white shirt, no tie. Like George Clooney in *Ocean's Eleven*. She would like that.

He was still tired, though. So he snorted a line off his kitchen counter. Tilted his head back and felt it course through him.

Yeahhhh . . . that was better. He felt almost immune. He put the vial of coke in his jacket packet. Cocktail waitresses and strippers always wanted drugs to lube them up.

In the lobby, he told the doorman not to wait up for him. The doorman did not respond.

Well, fuck him, Carson thought. Lowlife night man. One day people like that would know who he was.

The cab dropped him off at the hotel in Midtown. He looked up at the place and thought, *Christ, what a dump.* But she was just a cocktail waitress. What else could she afford? Probably she'd been here before. Probably she thought she was something. A black girl who was thin and tried to talk like she was white. He would enjoy telling the hedge-fund asshole about it the next day. *Yeah, you know what? That bitch called me. What do you think about that?* Tell the asshole that he could keep his numbers and algorithms and spreadsheets, Bill Carson knew how to read people.

He took the elevator to the eighth floor and walked down the hall to the room. He adjusted his shirt and checked his fly and knocked on the door.

Her name. Her name?

Sandra.

"Oh, Sandra? Sandra? It's me."

He knocked once more.

The door opened. Carson did not see the black girl in the doorway. What he saw was a white man. Before he could say anything, the German punched him in the face.

CHAPTER TWELVE

Miller hit him hard enough to knock him down. He crouched down next to him and grabbed him by the shirtfront and pulled him up and hit him again. Square in the nose. Then he pulled him into the hotel room.

Miller locked the door behind him. Then he put Carson into a chair. Carson came around and put things in focus.

"Oh God," he said. "You. I thought you were in prison."

"Early release," Miller said. "Good behavior."

"Oh . . . oh Jesus," Carson groaned. "I think my nose is broken."

"It is," Miller said. "You ever been to prison?"

"No. Seriously, I think my nose is broken."

"It won't kill you," Miller said. "You realize that filing a false criminal complaint is a felony?"

"I don't know what you're talking about." Carson looked around the room.

Miller said, "I know what you're thinking." Miller pulled his jacket lapel back so Carson could see the revolver tucked into his belt. "Call out for help and I'll kill you. Understand?"

"I understand. Where's the girl?"

Miller smiled. "You really thought she'd be here, didn't you? You are catnip to the ladies, uh?"

"Fucking whore."

Miller rapped the side of Carson's head with the gun. Enough to sting, enough to frighten, but not to injure.

"You listen to me very carefully," Miller said. "You go near that girl again, you try to get her in trouble at her workplace, you threaten or harm her in any way, I'll find you and I'll kill you. She doesn't need men like you in her life. Do we understand each other?"

". . . yes."

Miller brought a chair over and set it in front of Carson. Then he went to the sink and brought a white towel over to Carson and handed it to him.

"Here," Miller said.

Carson put the towel on his nose.

Miller said, "Tilt your head back so the bleeding will stop. . . . Yes, like that. . . . Now, last time I saw you, you said something about wanting to get me 'on the same page.' Do you remember that?"

"It was just talk."

"It was a threat," Miller said. "I didn't get on the same page with you and soon I was arrested. Tell me what you know about that."

"I don't know anything about it."

"You knew I was in prison. You said so just a minute ago."

"I . . . I was *told* that. I didn't have anything to do with it."

"You were there when Tanner threatened me. You were part of it."

"You're wasting your time. You can't prove me or Tanner had anything to do with your arrest."

"But you see, I don't have to prove it. I know Tanner set me up. This talk with you is not for the purpose of getting some sort of signed statement from you. It wouldn't do much good, as it would be obtained under duress. No, Carson. I'm here to find out what you know."

"I'm not going to help you."

"I picked this hotel in part because it's old-fashioned. It's got windows you can open. See? You don't cooperate with me, you go out the window. See?"

Carson turned to look at the window. It was lifted up about six inches. He could hear the traffic on the street below.

Carson turned back and said, "I don't think you'll do it."

"Young man," Miller said, "I've done it. I've done it to men who've done nothing personal to me whatsoever. If there's a hell, I'm going already. So what's one more man?"

"I—look, I can't tell you what I don't know."

Miller put the barrel of the Ruger against Carson's knee and said, "Let us assume you are correct about me. That I don't have the nerve to kill you. I pull this trigger and you'll lose that knee. It'll heal, but you'll limp the rest of your life. Knowing that very real possibility, why would you protect a man like Tanner?"

Carson said nothing. Miller pulled the hammer back on the pistol.

"All right, all right, don't! Look, it's not just Tanner. Tanner's just a free agent. He's a fixer, an independent contractor. I didn't authorize him to do what he did."

"You didn't authorize him to frame me?"

"No."

"But you know that he did."

"Yes. Fuck. Yes, I knew he did it. But it wasn't my idea. It was not done at my direction. Christ, Tanner wouldn't take orders from me. I'm just a grunt. A talking suit."

"I heard you talk quite a bit to your friend at the bar," Miller said. "Yes, I was there. You speak very loudly. From what I understood, you practically ran the State Department."

"Man, I didn't even have a title. I was just trying to impress that asshole."

"Is Tanner working for the CIA?"

"No. He used to, but now he's an independent security

consultant. Like I told you, a fixer."

"Who is he fixing for?"

"I don't know."

"If you don't stop lying to me, I'm going to maim you. Permanently."

"He works for Jay. Jay Gehlen. You know who that is, don't you?"

"No."

"Jay was undersecretary to the Secretary of State. Lindsey Horvath. I mean, you know who she is, don't you?"

Miller lowered the gun. Carson had just named the former Secretary of State. A woman who had resigned from that office eight months ago.

Miller said, "Lindsey Horvath?"

"Yes."

"The Secretary of State?"

"Yes."

"The daughter of the former Secretary of Defense?"

"Yes. The same one."

"And now she's running for President?"

"Yes."

Miller sat back, taking it in. A Presidential candidate. And, from what he'd read, a pretty formidable one.

Miller said, "Are you telling me the former Secretary of State ordered Tanner to have me put in jail?"

"I'm not saying she ordered it," Carson said. "These aren't stupid people, you know. They don't put things like that in written memos. I don't know what she said to Jay or what Jay said to her. But Tanner would have been acting under Jay's orders."

"But why?"

"Oh for Christ's sake, you know why. You were the turd in the proverbial punch bowl. You were in the way. Your report discredited Eightball, so we had to discredit your report in order to validate Eightball. We had to discredit you."

"So you could have your war."

"Yes. But it wasn't about you. The White House . . . the President . . . his office didn't want to go to war. He's a closet pacifist and maybe not all that closeted about it. He hates war. He ran campaigning against the Iraq War. The President was putting his stock in your stupid ass report to justify his indecision. He was clinging to it to justify his inaction. We needed to do something to push him over the line."

"We?"

"The State Department."

"You mean Ms. Horvath."

"Yeah. Same thing. It wasn't about you. Not really. The dispute wasn't between you and Tanner or you and me. It was a dispute between the State Department and the White House. Don't you see?"

"The White House didn't want a war in Syria, but Mr. Gehlen and Ms. Horvath did."

"Yes. Look, you don't understand. History was at stake. The President was fighting historical forces at work. The United States can't sit by and let men like Assad do whatever they want. We have to act. We have a duty. We have a global responsibility."

For the first time, Miller realized the young man was high or drunk. Probably both. Talking loosely and passionately about American destiny. Carson was no cynic, fueled only by ambition. Carson was a true believer. And the true believers were usually the most dangerous.

"So you decided to frame me."

"It wasn't anything personal," Carson said. "It's war, man. And it's not like we killed you or anything."

"Right. It's not like you killed me."

"Look man, you're German. You people once wanted to

dominate the world. You were all about enslaving and slaughtering. We're not like that."

"You're not the Third Reich."

Carson didn't catch the humor in it. He was stoned all right, Miller decided.

Carson said, "No, man. We're not interested in dominating the world. We're Americans. All we want to do is protect America."

"By bombing Syria?"

"Fuck yes!" Carson said. He didn't seem afraid anymore. Talk of his crusade had emboldened him. "If there's instability in the world, we have a duty, we have the *right* to assert ourselves. It's all part of the Project."

"The project?"

"Yes, the Restoration Project. We're restoring this country to what it once was. The President was in the way. He needed to be pointed in the right direction. He needed to be guided. I told you, he's indecisive. That's why we had to eliminate the uncertainties."

"And protect people like Rashid."

"Yes."

Miller thought for a moment. Then he said, "Rashid was working for your people all along, wasn't he? He wasn't planted by the Islamic State, was he?"

"I didn't say that."

"The smile on your face tells me I'm right."

Carson was still smiling. "And what if he was? How are you going to prove that?"

Miller thought about hitting the American again. Punch him hard enough to knock him off his chair. But Miller's hand was still sore from the last couple of punches, and using the gun might cause too much damage.

Miller said, "This Restoration Project you speak of, what is it about?"

Carson seemed back in his element. He believed he had gained some sort of advantage over the German by telling him that Eightball had been theirs all along. Now the German would understand what sort of power he was dealing with.

Carson said, "Our goals are simple. One, we defend our homeland. Two, we fight multiple wars in critical regions. Three, we promote regime change. Four, we use the United States military to exploit the revolution in military affairs."

"Well," Miller said, "I'm not sure what any of that means. I mean, promote regime change to what end?"

"Freedom."

Miller sighed. He realized he was talking to a fool. Miller said, "Freedom?"

"Yeah, go ahead and sneer. You Europeans are good at that. Just like you did in Germany when you tried to lecture us about Assad and the rebels. Laugh all you like, but we liberated Iraq. We liberated Syria from a tyrant."

"The liberator becomes the occupier. And then the occupier becomes the oppressor. That's the way it always works out, whether you intend it or not."

"At least we're doing something."

Miller stared at him. "You're doing something," Miller said. "Carson, have you ever worn a uniform yourself? Have you ever been in combat?"

"Well . . ."

"Have you ever been a soldier?"

"No," Carson said. "I serve my country in other ways." He seemed to believe it.

"Have you ever heard of a soldier named Cal Herndon?"

"No. Should I have?"

"Yes. He was an American. He was killed recently in Afghanistan, fighting a war for chicken-shit men like you."

"Well, I don't care if you hold me in contempt. The opinion of a German nihilist means nothing to me. Besides, there's nothing you can do about it now. The war's in motion. You couldn't stop it and you couldn't stop us."

Miller leaned back.

"I think you've misunderstood me," Miller said.

"How so?"

"I came to your country not to save it from misguided wars. Or from people like you and Tanner and Jay Gehlen. You can have your war."

Carson said, "What did you come here for?"

Miller said, "Compensation."

Carson lowered the washcloth from his nose. The washcloth now stained with blood. Carson said, "I don't understand."

"I don't care about your war," Miller said. "What I care about is what you took from me. You and your people stole something from me. And now you're going to pay it back. That's why I came here."

"Compensation? . . . You mean money?"

"Yes," Miller said. "I spent a year in prison and lost my career and pension. You've informed me that Ms. Horvath was behind it. So now you are going to go to Ms. Horvath and/or Mr. Gehlen and tell them they are to pay me for that. That will settle the dispute between us."

Carson stared at the German for a few moments. "Settle the dispute? You mean, pay you?"

"Yes."

"Pay you what?"

"I've calculated that I'm owed about a million dollars for my trouble. My losses. Compensation for lost wages, future and past, and damage to my reputation. One million dollars."

Carson stared some more. Then he said, "You're insane.

There's no way they're going to pay you that. You're talking about a million dollars."

"A small sum for ruining a man's livelihood," Miller said. "I know something about your country's political process. I suspect Ms. Horvath has raised well over a hundred million dollars in her campaign for the presidency. She can spare one percent of that."

"A million dollars . . . you can't . . . even if she could spare that, you think she's just going to hand it to you in a bag?"

"A suitcase will work," Miller said. "Probably you'll need two suitcases. A million dollars. A small sum to pay for your war and her political viability."

Carson said, "You think I'm going to call Jay Gehlen and tell him he has to give a million dollars of Lindsey Horvath's money to some crazy fucking German who says he wants to 'settle a dispute.' You really think I'm going to do that?"

Miller smiled and said, "Young man, by this time tomorrow, I have the utmost faith you will."

CHAPTER THIRTEEN

Jay Gehlen said, "Did he lose his job because of this?"

Tanner said, "Oh, yeah. He was arrested before I could get to New York to put a stop to it. The police did a test and found cocaine in his bloodstream. He also had about a .13 blood alcohol level. And they charged him with public indecency."

"But I thought you said he was tied to a tree? Why didn't he tell the police that he was tied there?"

"Maybe he tried to," Tanner said. "Hopefully, he didn't tell them too much. He claims he told me everything."

"Did it . . . affect him?"

"He was crying, yes. I mean, the man had been tied to a tree naked in Central Park. He was humiliated. It was almost noon before someone called the cops to let him loose. Out there all that time with his junk hanging out. Yeah, it fucked him up."

"What did he tell the police? Specifically."

"He said a hooker did it."

Gehlen said, "Well, that's a relief."

"Yeah, well," Tanner said, "he thinks he still has a job working for this campaign and a place in the Administration."

Gehlen shook his head. "That's out of the question. Lindsey will find out about this probably by tomorrow. In fact, I'll probably have to tell her about it. You know how she hates surprises."

Lindsey Horvath, Gehlen's current vessel to power, was in Iowa, securing a beachhead for the next caucus. She was looking better these days. Her recent surgery to perk up her drooping eyelids made her look less like a reptile. Gehlen hoped she would remember to wear her contact lenses because her glasses gave her the appearance of a mean-spirited Scottish schoolteacher.

Tanner said, "And will you tell her about the German too?"

Gehlen leaned back in his chair, thinking.

They were in Gehlen's office in Washington. It was a modest office, spare and undecorated. A few signed copies of books on the shelf, one of them by a Vice-President he had once worked for. Gehlen had written most of that book. He was a fair writer who would have made a good lawyer had he the slightest interest in law. He had graduated first in his class at Yale Law School, a couple of years behind the Clintons. The counter-culture had largely left the Ivy League by the time he got there. Of that he was glad. Gehlen thought the only good thing that came out of the sixties was *Star Trek*. He thought of the late sixties and early seventies as a low point in American history. A time when America had become unsure of itself and its place in the world. At Yale, he had argued that President Nixon was soft for not dropping nuclear weapons on North Vietnam. Seeing American servicemen scrambling to the helicopter on the rooftop of the American embassy during the fall of Saigon had left him enraged.

He was an unattractive man, short and puffy, and he was unable to smile without it looking like a sneer. But this didn't matter much to him. He was not vain, not about his appearance anyway. And he had never pined for elective office. He knew from an early age that he would be the one pulling the levers behind the electable. As a boy, his biblical hero had been Joseph, counselor to the Pharaoh.

His critics said that he was in love with war. Or the idea of war, and they always pointed out that he himself had never actually fought in one. These attacks never bothered him. He always said he was an advocate of "Peace through Strength."

He had a knack, perhaps even a gift, for attaching himself to those in power. For persuading them that they needed him more than he needed them. After his Vice-President's political career fizzled, he gravitated to Hermann Horvath and worked for him when Horvath ran the Department of Defense. It was during that time he formed a close relationship with Horvath's daughter, Lindsey.

Now Tanner was asking Gehlen if Lindsey knew about the German they had sent to prison. The answer was, *of course* she knew. She had known from the beginning. It was funny how Tanner thought sometimes. Like a woman wouldn't be capable of taking part in such things. Tanner was old school. A chauvinist.

Gehlen said, "Well, the point is, she'll have to know what happened to Carson. I think we have, at best, twenty-four hours before the media gets a hold of this. A former aide to Secretary of State Horvath found naked and incoherent in Central Park is something that's going to be newsworthy. But she'll be ready. She'll distance herself, but also show compassion and say that he's very sick and troubled and deserves our prayers."

"But what about Carson? What if he decides to talk to the press?"

"Carson's not going to do that. He's not stupid. He wants to come back in the circle and he knows if he talks, that's not going to happen. We'll give him some money, keep his head above water. Let him think a job is waiting for him after Lindsey gets elected."

"But you said that was out of the question."

"It's very much out of the question. But he doesn't know that," Gehlen said. "This German, though. What do you make of him?"

Tanner said, "He wants a million dollars."

"You told me that," Gehlen said. "But do you think he's serious? Or is he just crazy?"

"I think he's serious. I met him and he seemed sane to me. An asshole, but not crazy."

"You met him just the one time?"

"Yeah."

"What did you think?"

"I didn't think he was very much. Another desk man at German intelligence."

Gehlen said, "You said that Carson told you the German knew about Eightball. Knew that we planted him. How did he find that out?"

"It's possible Carson lied to me about that," Tanner said. "I mean, it's possible that Carson told him, but wants me to think the German figured it out on his own. I guess it doesn't matter either way."

"It matters to me," Gehlen said. "You work for us, you give us complete loyalty. If I find out Carson gave that information away, I'll finish him."

You mean, *I'll* finish him, Tanner thought. Tanner said, "If it's what you want."

"No," Gehlen said, "hold off on that for now."

"Well," Tanner said, "what do you want to do?"

Gehlen made a temple of his hands. "We should have killed him last year."

"We couldn't do that," Tanner said. "We agreed he had to be discredited. Tarnish him, tarnish his report."

"Yeah, but we should have found some way to tarnish him *and* kill him. It's my fault. I should have thought it out more. I didn't think he would figure out we set him up."

"He had a long time to think," Tanner said.

"It was bad luck," Gehlen said. "Bad luck that he was the one who was ordered to interview Rashid. They could have picked ten other desk jockeys to interview Rashid and he would have been fine. But the Germans picked this guy to interview Rashid and he smelled a rat. Bad luck."

"He didn't know Eightball was planted by us, though. Not initially. I don't think he figured that out until he talked to Carson."

"Well, now he does know. Or at least he thinks he does. That's why we can't pay him. We can't let this guy run around when he knows these things about us. About Lindsey. It's a matter of national security. Are we on the same page?"

"Absolutely," Tanner said. He was smiling now, relieved. "You can't negotiate with these people." Tanner had avoided saying, *you can't negotiate with terrorists.* He thought that might have been a little too much, even for Gehlen.

"Okay, we're agreed," Gehlen said. "Contact him and let him think we're going to pay him. When he shows up to collect it, kill him."

"You think he'll show?"

"For a million dollars, yeah, he'll show. What else has he got to do?"

CHAPTER FOURTEEN

Hayes bought a large coffee, a sweet roll, and a *Wall Street Journal* at a shop near Bryant Park. He added lots of cream and sugar to the coffee and tucked the newspaper under his arm. He was a tall man with a swimmer's build. He wore glasses and a blue Brooks Brothers suit with brown twill and he carried an attaché case. He looked like any other lawyer or bond trader in Manhattan. The glasses were cosmetic, not corrective. His vision was still 20/20, the same as it had been when he was a Special Forces sniper.

He walked the perimeter of Bryant Park, passing by the New York Library before he completed the square. At times he looked at the tables on the west end. Then he looked up at the apartment building on the opposite side of the park.

Twenty minutes later, he was inside the building and on the eighth floor. He picked his way into an apartment. It was empty as he had expected. He propped a chair against the front door and walked through the apartment. The apartment was clean and well kept. In the kitchen he saw a picture of the couple who owned it. Two men, posing for their wedding announcement in the *New York Times*. It was a weekday and they would both be at work. Hopefully neither of them would come back to the apartment for the next three hours because then he would have to kill them.

He found a window he liked in the bedroom. He opened the window and the sounds of traffic and the city drifted inside. He looked out onto the park. It was a nice day, the air crisp and cool, sun coming through the clouds. He opened the attaché case and began to piece together the sections of the rifle. He put the scope on last, screwing it into place with the small screwdriver that came with the case.

Hayes checked his watch. He put the receptive device in his ear that would connect him to a device attached to the cuff of Tanner's coat. Tanner would be meeting the German at the table on the other side of Bryant Park in two hours and thirteen minutes. Tanner had told him the mark would be on time. Tanner said the Germans were always punctual.

Hayes would be ready for him. He removed the sweet roll from the paper bag and took a satisfying bite out of it.

Tanner came fifteen minutes early. He took a seat at the table in Bryant Park and panned the area. He didn't expect to see the German and he didn't. Tanner plugged a set of earphones into what looked like a regular iPhone. He brought his hand to his chin and said into his sleeve, "I don't see him."

Hayes's voice came into Tanner's headset. Hayes said, "I don't either. Though I don't have much in the way of description."

"A white male of about forty. Maybe he'll be dressed like a European."

"If he's stupid," Hayes said, peering down from the high-rise window.

Tanner said, "He'll be here."

Tanner thought of the time when he was about the age Hayes was and he had shot and killed a labor leader in Central America on his way to see his mistress. That mark had been punctual.

Ten minutes passed, then another five, and the German didn't show. Another ten minutes passed and Tanner began to wonder if Carson had bungled the setup. He had told Carson what to say to the German, where to meet. Tanner had told Carson, "If he believes he's got money coming to him, he'll get reckless. They usually do."

Carson was a mess. The German had left him naked in Central Park and humiliated him. Carson had gotten into politics because he was mean and ambitious and believed he was meant to be a great man who was going to make his mark in the world. Carson had never expected anything like this. Carson had said, "I'd like to be there when you kill him." And Tanner had to suppress a laugh at the bullshit. Carson trying to get back some of his manhood, talking tough. Now Tanner wondered if Carson had been dumb enough to make face-to-face contact with the German and let the German shake the truth out of him. Carson would be too stupid and arrogant to realize that he was disposable.

A shabby-looking woman drifted over to Tanner's table. She smelled and had bad teeth and straggly hair. She was pushing a shopping cart full of aluminum cans. She lingered by his table for a moment. Tanner took her in at a glance and then ignored her.

She came closer to the table and said, "You look like the D.A."

Tanner raised his head and said, "Excuse me?"

"You look like the D.A."

Tanner said, "D.A.?"

"Drastic asshole," she said. Her face sort of wobbled.

"Beat it," Tanner said.

The woman took a cell phone out of her dirty coat and chucked it on the table. She resumed pushing her cart of cans and shuffled away, the wheels of the cart crunching on the ground.

Tanner looked at the cell phone the woman had left on the table. It was a cheap ghetto phone, the type used by street-corner drug dealers.

Hayes's voice came into the headset.

"What was that about?"

"Nothing," Tanner said. "A transient."

"What did she put on the table?"

The cell phone rang.

Tanner flinched. For a brief moment he thought the old bag had put a bomb in front of him. But that didn't make sense.

"Carl," Hayes said.

The cell phone rang again.

"Shut up," Tanner said and took the earpiece out of his left ear. The cell phone rang a third time before he answered it.

"Yeah," Tanner said.

"Mr. Tanner."

Tanner smiled. "Herr Miller. I've been waiting for you. You get stuck in traffic?"

"Not exactly," Miller said. "You're familiar with Dien Bien Phu, aren't you?"

Tanner said, "A little before my time. That was where the Vietnamese commies knocked the hell out the French, right?"

"That's right."

"From what I understood," Tanner said, "there were quite a few krauts there too. Ex Waffen SS who had joined the French Foreign Legion to avoid getting hanged in Germany."

Miller said, "You know your history."

"Part of the trade," Tanner said. "Don't tell me, your daddy was one of the soldiers who fought there."

"If he had, I wouldn't be here. You know what the Legion forgot?"

"What's that?"

"That you should never gather forces on a plain at the foot of a mountain," Miller said. "Valleys attract invaders."

Tanner said, "No mountains here, Miller."

"No, just a lot of tall buildings. Maybe you've got a sniper in one of them. Maybe more than one."

Tanner said, "Now, that wouldn't be very nice."

"No, it wouldn't."

"I suppose you don't want to meet me here, then."

"No."

"What do we do, then? Sit here and talk about the incompetence of the French?"

"Yes, the Americans did much better in Vietnam."

"We could have if the politicians had allowed it," Tanner said. "Look, you're the one who wanted to meet."

"I want to live too," Miller said. "More than once, I've seen you talk into your sleeve."

Tanner looked around the park. The German could see him. But where the fuck was the German?

"So I brought backup," Tanner said. "Why shouldn't I? You might want to kill me."

"I might," Miller said, "but I don't. You will remove your coat and the headset and leave those devices at the table. Keep the new phone with you. You will walk to the subway and get on the 9 to Brooklyn. If and when I feel you are alone, I will join you on the train."

"And then what?"

"Then we discuss terms. Wasn't that what you wanted?"

"We're reasonable people," Tanner said.

Tanner boarded the train and went through two stops. There were too many people on the subway. Tanner didn't like it, but he still had the compact Glock .40 in his jacket. He had left his overcoat and headset at the park. He could kill the German on the train and slip off. Or he could claim that the German was trying to kill him and that he had acted in self-defense. It could be messy, but Tanner was comfortable with a certain amount of mess.

At the third stop, the cell phone rang again.

"Yeah."

Miller said, "Get off at the next stop."

"I thought you wanted to talk on the train."

"I changed my mind."

"I guess I shouldn't be surprised." Tanner looked up and down the length of his car. A couple of Hispanic kids. A woman in a business suit wearing tennis shoes, her briefcase on the seat next to her. Other passengers looking straight ahead, avoiding eye contact as necessary. He couldn't see much through the doors to the other cars.

Tanner said, "Are you on this train? I can find out, you know."

"I'm sure you can, superspy," Miller said and clicked off.

Tanner got off the train at the next stop. He walked into a thick crowd of people and smelled the faint stench of urine and humanity. More people avoiding eye contact. But Tanner looked at them all, looked for the German. Hayes and the other man he had brought to the park were not here with him. Tanner was okay with that. He had not thought much of the German when he met him and he still didn't. Tanner still had the gun in his jacket. It would be good to find the German in the crowd. Maybe get in next to him and stick the gun in his chest and fire and then melt into the crowd. He'd done that sort of thing before.

The cell phone rang again and Tanner answered it.

Miller said, "Get on the 3 going to 14th."

Miller clicked off and Tanner moved to the train. He got on when the doors opened and took a seat.

There were only a few people in the car with him. More commuters, faceless, expressionless, hiding behind their newspapers, a couple of them reading the fashionable thrillers. New

Yorkers taking refuge in what they thought was culture.

The train jerked then began rolling, the pitch rising. Tanner stayed where he was, watching the darkness through the window blur by.

The door to the next car opened and a uniformed transit cop came through it. The transit cop moved slowly, looking at the seats. Tanner looked at the window again, blending in with the others. The transit cop reached the door to the next car and pulled it open. Then he was gone.

Then the door slid open again and the German came through it.

Tanner looked at him, was still processing it when Miller said, "Ah, Mr. Tanner. What are the odds of running into you?"

Tanner looked at the other people in the car. The German came toward him, but stayed out of grabbing distance. The German sat on the other side of the train, facing Tanner. The German was in a raincoat, his hands still in his pockets. Tanner could see the bulge in the raincoat, the end of a gun pointing at him.

Miller said, "Let's see. Last I heard, you were working in Washington."

Tanner motioned with his head toward the coat and said, "I see you came prepared."

Miller said, "I see you didn't bring my money."

"I thought we should talk first."

"About what?"

"About this misunderstanding," Tanner said. "Carson says you have this crazy idea we put you in jail."

"Carson confirmed it."

"People under duress will say anything. Surely, you would understand that."

"He didn't need duress. The big mouths usually don't."

"That's often the case," Tanner said. "But be that as it may, we're not bound by what he told you. He was not authorized to accept your offer."

"How about you? Are you authorized to settle this claim? Or just authorized to have someone shoot me?"

"You presume you're worth killing," Tanner said. "But you're no one. A convicted criminal, spouting conspiracy theories. You're nothing to me."

"Then why are you here?"

"I'm here to tell you to go home. Go back to Germany where you belong. Stay out of my country."

"Now that's pretty funny coming from you. Stay out of my country. Like you are the sheriff and this is your county?"

"That's right."

"But Mr. Tanner, you came to my country and made a ruin of my life. You did that at the request of Mr. Gehlen, huh? And maybe Ms. Horvath too."

"I don't work for them," Tanner said.

"Of course. You are an 'independent security consultant,' uh? But were you working for them when you killed Posner?"

Tanner smiled. "You've got a wild imagination. And a big mouth. Say we don't pay you. What then? What I mean is, what leverage do you have?"

"The leverage is Ms. Horvath. She wants to be President. That's not likely to happen if people become aware she was party to a murder. Not even in this country."

"This country," Tanner said. "You have something against this country, don't you? You think we should stay out of the Middle East, let dictators rule."

"I told Carson and I believe I told you last year, I don't care if you want a war. You have it now and now your sons are being killed in Syria at the rate of about thirty a day. You want to tell yourself that's a good thing for America, be my guest. But you took something from me, Tanner. You and your gang. And now you're going to pay it back."

"Or what?" Tanner said. "Or you'll go to *The New York Times* and tell them a story? Who will believe you?"

"No, I'll go to the European press and tell them. And it will trickle back to your newspapers. In time, it will. Not because you put a German citizen in prison. No one will care about that except me. But you killed an American, Tanner. Not just Posner, but a liquor store clerk as well. And when Gehlen and Ms. Horvath are threatened with the prospect of that going public, they'll turn on you and save themselves. People like that always do."

The door slid open again and the transit cop came back into the car. Miller stood up and said to Tanner, "Or didn't you know that?"

Miller followed the transit cop to the next car and got off at the next stop.

CHAPTER FIFTEEN

The governor of the Midwestern state was a small man with pig eyes and an oversized head. He was known for buying expensive suits that were too big for him. His name was Jerry Oates and he liked to be called Rowdy, the name he had given himself in college. Now he was sitting in a trailer in the southern part of his state facing a woman he thought was the embodiment of evil and wishing he wasn't afraid of her.

Lindsey Horvath, at fifty-two, was not an ugly woman. In her younger days, she could have passed for handsome. But even then she had the look of an earnest, mean-spirited Catholic nun. Time had only hardened the lines. Physically, she was plain and unapproachable. Men had never been drawn to her. Not for her looks. This was something that had never bothered her. Power in the form of sensuality was never something she had desired.

Lindsey had told Governor Oates that he was to leave his entourage outside. Oates smiled uneasily and said, "But it's raining."

"That's not my problem," Lindsey said, not smiling. And Oates went to the door of the trailer and told his aides and the Trooper detail to go sit in their cars.

He came back and Lindsey got straight down to business.

"I understand you had lunch with Jim Merchant last week," Lindsey said.

Big Jim Merchant was a senator from Florida. A man so

named because of his considerable height and charisma. Big Jim liked to say he was for the little man. He had recently been giving speeches saying that the little man wasn't being heard in Washington. Nothing new for a politician, but he knew how to sell it.

Jerry Oates wondered how Lindsey knew of his lunch with Big Jim. They both had taken steps to keep it secret. But then Lindsey had spies all over the country.

Oates smiled and said, "Sure I did. We both like to eat."

"Well, I like to eat too, Jerry. But I have to tell you I'm not comfortable with this."

"Why is that, Lindsey?"

Ah, a little backbone from the governor. It surprised Lindsey. But she knew it wouldn't last.

She said, "It concerns me because Big Jim is considering backing Tommy Nauls in the primary. Florida is a big state. You remember what it meant in 2000."

"It's not my state," Oates said.

"I understand that," Lindsey said, and here she did smile. It reminded Jerry Oates of a bully he knew in high school who would grin just before he hit you. Lindsey said, "I understand Florida is not your state. But if people think you're siding with Big Jim in this upcoming election, they might make the mistake of thinking you're supporting Nauls too. Do you understand me, now?"

"Yes, ma'am." Oates regretted having answered so quickly.

"It's a question of perception," Lindsey said.

"Yes."

Lindsey stared at Oates for a few awful moments. Then said, "Perception. It makes Washington wonder whose side you're on in this thing."

Oates straightened his back and said, "I wasn't aware the leash was that tight." He tried to smile again. He hoped that she would make a joke then and try to de-escalate the situation.

"It's that tight, Jerry."

Oates frowned and said, "I'm afraid you're going to have to be a little more specific."

"I'll make it as plain as I can. You are to contact Big Jim and tell him you're on board with me. You are to do that today. You will also tell him that it would be very ill-advised for him to throw his support behind Nauls."

"Madam," Oates said. He stopped. He had once addressed her as Madame Secretary, from her days at State. He had slipped and said it now because she had angered him. And scared him. He started again and said, "Lindsey. First of all, you haven't even formally declared your candidacy for President. Second, I never told you I would give you my unqualified support."

"You supported me when you were in Congress."

"Yes. But that was a long time ago. You know how things change."

"I guess you don't understand the position you're in, do you?"

"Tell me what position I'm in."

"Jerry," she said and smiled again. "Come on. We're old friends. I know what you did years ago. I don't judge you for it. But others may not be as understanding as I am."

The Midwestern governor shifted in his seat. "What are you talking about?"

"Oh come on, Jerry. Don't shit a shitter. I'm talking about the Hillerman Expressway."

Jerry Oates raised his hand to his face.

"Ah . . . what do you mean?"

Lindsey barked out a laugh. "Jerry! Jerry, come on. We both know what you did. You bought land outside of Indianapolis for about fifty grand, using a secret trust, and then you pushed a

$300 million appropriation bill through a closed-door Congressional budget conference. Six months later you sold that land at a $4 million profit."

"That's . . . ah . . ."

"Jerry, you went into Congress as an underpaid radio host and came out a millionaire. I know all about it."

"It was . . . ah . . . that was an investment. There were other people involved."

"Right," Lindsey said. "Well, when the Justice Department starts investigating your investment, you're going to find those other people aren't going to do shit for you. You'll be all alone. And you'll need all that money to pay for legal fees."

"You wouldn't . . ."

"Yes, Jerry. I would. I know who to call."

There was a long awful silence. Lindsey never took her eyes off the governor.

Then Oates said, "Listen, Lindsey. You know you can count on me."

"All the way?"

"All the way."

"And you'll make that call today."

"Yes, I'll call Jim today."

"Good," Lindsey said. She crossed the trailer to shake his hand. She held his hand after he was ready to release it and said, "Listen, I need your help, you know."

"Of, of course."

"I'd like you to be campaign chairman for this state."

"Okay."

"But we won't make an announcement yet. As you said, I haven't formally declared."

"Right."

"It would mean a lot to me," she said.

"Of course."

"And Jerry? I'll need you to make a donation too. You know, as a gesture of good faith."

Jerry Oates stared at her.

"How much?"

"Oh, nothing too heavy. About two hundred should do it." She smiled without showing her teeth. "You know how expensive advertising is."

"Two hundred thousand?"

"Yes. I'll have someone pick it up tomorrow. Off the books, you understand."

"I understand."

The governor slunk out the door into the rain.

Jay Gehlen ran into him outside the trailer and said hello. Governor Oates didn't say hello back, not feeling particularly Rowdy then. He just walked off, giving an angry signal to his troops that they were leaving. Gehlen smiled after him. Lindsey often left people like that.

In the trailer, Gehlen said, "He didn't seem very happy."

"He's a fag," Lindsey said. It was a term she used often around people she knew wouldn't tell on her. Gehlen was one of those people. Her use of the word was strange to Gehlen, considering. But she never said it in public. Another one of her favorite private expressions was motherfucker.

Lindsey regarded Gehlen without expression and said, "Well?"

Gehlen said, "Is this place secure?"

"Yeah, I had security sweep it this afternoon for bugs. Go ahead and give me the bad news."

"How do you know it's bad?"

"Because I know you. The German's still alive, isn't he?"

"Yeah."

"Christ. What is it with you people? Does your target have to be in Latin America for you to shoot him?"

"He was in New York. It wasn't that easy."

"He's an enemy of the State. A man convicted of a crime. How hard should it be to make someone like that disappear?"

"They were on a crowded subway. Tanner didn't have an opportunity."

"So now what? I have to hire more bodyguards? Bodyguards cost money. Are you going to pay for that?"

Gehlen said, "I know what that costs. Tanner can get us more men. But he wouldn't have to, we wouldn't have to do that, if you'd formally declare your candidacy. Then Secret Service would assign a detail to protect you."

"I'm not ready to formally declare."

Jesus Christ, Gehlen thought. It was silly. Not ready to formally declare. For God's sake, the whole country knew she was running for President.

Gehlen said, "Perhaps now would be a good time. I can help you write the speech."

"I don't need your help for that," she said. "I'll declare when I'm ready. And not because some whacko kraut's trying to extort money from me."

"I'm not suggesting we pay the man," Gehlen said. "I never suggested that."

"I didn't say you were." Lindsey paused. She knew she couldn't push Gehlen around too much. He had put his political chips on her to take the White House and give him more power than he'd ever had before. But Gehlen was tough too and he wouldn't be much good to her emasculated and indecisive. Lindsey was savvy enough to know that.

In a softer tone, Lindsey said, "Look, it's just not the right time. Okay?"

Gehlen could ask her why it wasn't the right time. And she would tell him that federal regulations would kick in and require that equal time be given to other candidates on television and radio, and that there would be closer examination of her fund-raising. But he would know that was all so much horseshit. The real reason was that if Lindsey formally declared her candidacy, she would likely face pressure from the media and other candidates about the fees she charged for speeches. Last week, she had been paid $250,000 to speak at a cosmetics company in Chicago. The week before that, $200,000 at a natural gas company in Texas. Lindsey wasn't ready to give up those speaking fees yet.

Add to that, she had never liked Secret Service agents. She said they weren't "loyal" enough. Lindsey was big on loyalty. A Secret Service agent would give his life for hers, but he couldn't be counted on to murder a pesky German agent who was making her life difficult.

Lindsey said, "What happened in New York?"

"Tanner laid a trap for the German and it didn't work. The German got him alone, on the subway, like I said."

"Did he hurt Tanner?"

"No. He just talked to him. He told Tanner that he thinks Tanner killed Posner. He threatened us with that. Ma'am, he threatened *you* with that."

"He says I ordered Posner killed?"

"Not in those words, but I think that was the drift."

"Well, that's nothing he can prove. The man was killed in a liquor store."

"He told Tanner he'd take it to the German press."

"Would that resonate here? If the German press listened to him, I mean?"

"Possibly. Not likely. They've said worse things about Bush. You can always find some left-wing rag to say something. Usually, it doesn't go anywhere."

"It wouldn't go anywhere," Lindsey said. "But that's not the point. This motherfucker's threatening me now. How did he trace this to me?"

"I don't know."

"Well, that's just fucking great, you don't know. Why didn't you just kill this guy last year?"

"I told you, we couldn't do that. We had to discredit him."

"Well, good job on the discrediting. But don't you think you should have gone a little farther than that? I mean, do I have to tell you everything?"

"No, ma'am."

Lindsey sighed. "Is he asking for more now?"

"No. He still just wants the million."

"That's it? Just a million?"

"It's a lot for one man."

"It's nothing," Lindsey said. "It'd pay for about three days' advertising in Virginia. What I mean is, if this guy really believes I ordered him to be framed and that I ordered some gutless bureaucrat to be killed, don't you think he would ask for more?"

"Tanner said he just wants to be compensated for what we took from him."

"What *we* took from *him*? What about what he's doing to *us*? I'm trying to protect freedom. We are the guardians of the general good. Of order and security. Who is this man that he should stop us? Who's he working for?"

"I don't think he's working for anyone," Gehlen said. "I don't know that the money, or the amount of money, matters that much to him. It seems just like a point of pride to him."

"Point of pride?" Lindsey laughed. "Point of pride. Christ, you talk as if he's someone who fixed my toilet and I stiffed him on the bill. I'm trying to run a country here. National security is at stake and some America-hating douchebag wants me to pay him a debt. What do we do next? Free all the prisoners at Guantanamo and give them fifty grand a piece? Tell them no hard feelings and they can go back to killing Jews and American soldiers? It's crazy."

"I agree, ma'am."

"Well, I hope you do. Do you remember what I said when you came on board with me?"

"Well . . . we talked about a lot of things."

"I told you then that I need you to be the sharp point of my spear. You told me then that you would do it. Did you mean it, Jay?"

"I meant it."

"Or were you just telling me what I wanted to hear?"

"I meant what I said."

"Good. As far as I'm concerned, this man is a terrorist and a threat to our nation and I'm not going to give him a penny. Tell Tanner to finish it."

She thought about Gehlen after he left. She knew she had been short with him, but she also knew he could take it. She knew she needed Gehlen. Gehlen had a feel for the battle, something her father had told her was important in politics. Gehlen was a stayer. Gehlen had a brain and could have made a fortune on Wall Street or even in Silicon Valley, if he'd wanted. But that sort of existence would have been intolerable for him. If not for politics, he would die of boredom. Lindsey knew this and exploited it. Gehlen wasn't a fag. Not sexually or otherwise. Gehlen had the qualities she sought in a lieutenant: smooth, cold, and black of heart. A pit bull who would tear someone's throat out if Lindsey snapped her fingers. That was what mattered.

Lindsey Horvath was not someone who thought about people in terms of their sexuality, except to the degree she could exploit it. When she began her political career, she had said she was firmly opposed to gay marriage when the truth was she didn't feel one way or another about it. Then the cultural tide changed and the courts started ruling for the gays and she rolled with it and eased the subject out of her speeches. She understood her party's obsession with cultural issues and said what they wanted to hear. But, like Nixon, she felt that foreign policy should take precedence over domestic issues. History didn't much care where you stood on domestic issues. History noted what your achievements were in foreign policy. FDR's management of the Second World War. Kennedy's handling of the Cuban Missile Crisis. Reagan in Berlin saying, *"Tear down this wall!"*

Self-awareness is not a trait commonly found in most politicians. And this was generally the case with Lindsey Horvath. Before being Defense Secretary, her father had been a senator during the Nixon administration and had supported Nixon almost to the day Nixon resigned in disgrace. Lindsey spent most of her childhood in Washington, going to exclusive schools and living in a tony neighborhood. But she insisted to all who would listen that she was a simple country girl from Hastings, Nebraska, the town where her parents had grown up. She had been doing it for so long that she had convinced herself it was true.

Her father said that Nixon hadn't done anything worse than Kennedy or Johnson or even that sainted prick Roosevelt, but Nixon had the bad luck of being a man without charm. Lindsey's father said that Nixon had understood that the most important thing was to win. For the family Horvath, Nixon's sin was not that he had bombed Cambodia and Laos too much, but that he hadn't done it enough. Lindsey believed wholeheartedly the revisionist fiction that the Vietnam War was a noble cause and could have been won if the United States had just tried harder. She said these things on cable news often. She defended the use of torture, though always using the politician's term "enhanced interrogation." She rarely lost debates because she never doubted she was right. She had never struggled with self-doubt and scorned those who did.

Her genuine belief—shared by many liberals as well as conservatives—was that God had destined America to lead the world. For her, American exceptionalism was a given. The President she had served—or worked with—spoke of American exceptionalism, but Lindsey could tell he didn't really believe it. That was his problem, really. He was not sure of himself, not sure of his country. He had no real conviction. Lindsey had no time for that sort of ambivalence. You were either on the bus or off.

She thought about her father now. He had died a few years ago. And though she missed him, she knew she had been to some degree liberated by his passing. No one would be able to second-guess her. Now that he was gone, she would go further than he had.

The old man had claimed to have stormed the beaches at Normandy, but Lindsey later learned he had fabricated that. He had actually been working as an army supply clerk in London on D-Day. This truth didn't upset her. If the old man had wanted to sell himself as a war hero, that was his business. It was what his constituents wanted to hear. The old man spoke passionately about his military service whenever the subject of Vietnam came up. He had said that the students protesting the Vietnam War were traitors and should have been shot for treason. And this was a view Lindsey came to share. Like the old man, she thought Ford was weak for pardoning the draft-dodgers who had fled to Canada. At a minimum, the draft-dodgers should not have been allowed to return to the States. They had betrayed their country in a time of war. They had forfeited their right to citizenship and maybe even their right to live.

This was how Lindsey viewed the German. He was a traitor to western civilization. An enemy alien. They had tried to be reasonable with him. They had let him live, and now he was in their country demanding compensation. Demanding that she pay him for his trouble. It was brazen. If he had stayed in his own country, they would have let him alone and forgotten about him. But he had come to their country and made a claim. It was his decision, Lindsey thought. He had chosen to die.

CHAPTER SIXTEEN

Sandra Slay rode her scooter up to the comedy club where she worked on Thursday nights. She parked the bike and locked it. She took her helmet off and shook her hair. She looked over at the man standing near the entrance.

Sandra smiled in spite of herself and said, "Are you following me?"

Miller said, "Sorry. I just wanted to talk to you for a moment. If that's all right."

Sandra said, "I made the mistake of telling you I worked here too, didn't I?"

"I like to think it was not a mistake."

"I'm too trusting," the black girl said. "That's my problem. Well, come on in. I have to start my shift."

The German followed her in. Sandra took her place behind the bar. She asked Miller if he would like a Bass Ale and Miller said he'd prefer a cup of coffee. It was only six o'clock. Miller asked if it was too much trouble to make the coffee.

"No," she said. "The comedians, most of them don't drink. They need coffee to get through the night's work. They do runs. I mean, they'll perform here and then rush out to do another gig across town at the Comedy Store or the Improv. They work hard, man. All of them hoping they'll be the next Seinfeld."

"Who's that?"

The black girl stared at the German for a moment. "I forget you're not from here," she said.

"Because I sound like an American?"

"Hardly."

Miller said, "I'll try not to take too much of your time. I know you're busy. I wanted to give you something for helping me."

He put five one hundred dollar bills on the bar.

Sandra looked at the money for a moment. She frowned and pushed it back toward him. "Thanks all the same," she said.

Miller said, "You act like I've insulted you."

"You have. I don't like to be bought."

"That's not what I meant."

"I helped you, okay? I shouldn't have, but I did. I was pissed off at your friend and I let it get the better of me. I shouldn't have."

"He was not my friend."

"What did you do to that man, anyway?"

"I just talked with him."

"Talked to him, huh? Well, he hasn't been back at the bar since. You must have done something."

"He hasn't been back?"

"Not once."

"And you're okay with that, uh?"

"Yes, I'm okay with it, but . . . look, I'm not looking for a man to protect me. I'm not looking for a boyfriend. You came along when you knew I was angry and you . . . you exploited it. I've been thinking about it for the last couple of days and I don't like myself very much for lending myself to whatever it is you did. For all I know, you might have killed that man."

"I didn't do that."

"So what then? You ran him off because he tried to treat me like a prostitute? Am I supposed to be grateful to you for that?"

"No."

"But you did that after you 'talked' with him. After you got what you needed from him. You only threatened him to stay away from me because you felt you should. It doesn't change the fact that you used me, Mr. Miller. I don't like being used."

Miller put the money back into his jacket.

"You're right," he said. "I'm sorry."

"You're sorry. What do I do if he comes back? What do I do if he comes back and tells my boss that I got some German guy to beat him up and I get fired? What do I do then?"

"You find another job."

"Man, you are cold. Do you know how hard it is to find a job that pays that well? Short hours, big tips?"

"How long do you want to work in bars? How long do you want to tolerate men like that?"

"At least till I finish nursing school. And where do you get off telling me what I should be doing for a living?"

"You asked the question and I answered it. I meant no offense."

She looked at him for a while. "No, I suppose you didn't." She sighed. "You're a strange man. Or maybe you're just European. You don't belong here."

"That's what I hear," the German said. "Look, I am sorry that I used you to get at that man. You did not deserve it. Do you still have the number I gave you?"

"Yes."

"If anyone bothers you because of me, I want you to call me immediately. I don't think they will, but . . ."

"But what?"

Miller stood up. "But nothing. Thank you for helping me."

He started to go.

Sandra Slay said, "Wait a minute. Are you in some kind of trouble?"

"I wouldn't call it trouble."

"Right," she said, smiling. "God knows I don't need another

126

man in my life who says he's not in trouble. Do you know anyone in New York?"

"Not really."

"And you're white."

It perplexed Miller, her saying that. But Sandra Slay seemed to think it was funny for some reason.

Then she said, "And we're both lonely."

"I don't understand," Miller said.

"Neither do I," she said.

The girl looked at Miller for a long time without saying anything. It had been a long time since a woman had looked at him that way. Miller had been attracted to the girl from the moment he first saw her. Her smile, her skin, her neck, the way she talked . . . he liked all of her. He liked her more the more he saw her. He had not stopped to ask himself if she might feel something for him.

Sandra Slay said, "My shift ends at midnight. If you want to come back."

"I'd like that," Miller said.

Sandra Slay said, "I'm still a little angry at you, though. What I'm saying is, I might change my mind."

Miller said, "You might not."

When her shift ended, Miller offered her a ride home in the Jaguar. She said she didn't want to leave her scooter at the comedy club. She asked if he could leave his car there and ride on the back of the scooter behind her. Miller looked at her and realized she was serious. He agreed to it.

She lived in Brooklyn. Miller felt better when they crossed the bridge, the tension of Manhattan behind them. It was a strange sensation, riding across the Brooklyn Bridge on the back of this stranger's motor scooter, his hands on this girl's shoulders. The air blowing cold on his skin, the sounds of the scooter engine and the traffic around them. At some point, the girl reached up and guided his hand to her stomach. Miller put his arms around her and held on.

When they got to her apartment, Miller was still feeling aroused by the ride and the feel of her body. Miller looked at the couch, but kept his jacket and coat on. He felt confused. He had been married too long. He had been in jail too long.

Sandra Slay said, "I have to take a shower."

Miller pointed at the couch. "Is it okay if I sleep here?"

"I'll be out in a minute," she said. "Just go ahead and get in the bed."

That was all she said before she left him.

Miller took off his coat and jacket, folded them, and put them on the couch. In the bedroom, he stripped down to his shorts and undershirt and climbed into the bed. He left the bedside lamp on.

On the girl's nightstand were magazines and a copy of *The Ordeal of Change*. Ah, he thought. She was a fan of Hoffer. The German longshoreman turned philosopher. It might explain things.

He heard the shower water stop. Then he heard her brushing her teeth. He wondered where he was. He wondered how he had ended up in a pretty girl's apartment in Brooklyn, USA.

Sandra Slay came into the bedroom, wearing a shortie bathrobe. Her hair was damp and there were water beads on her neck. Christ, Miller thought. She was something to behold. She looked at him and he looked back at her.

She said, "Would you turn off the light, please?"

Miller turned off the light. Some light still came in through the partially opened door. She turned around and slipped off the bathrobe and hung it on a hook. Miller saw her naked backside briefly before she closed the door and the room went black. Then she crossed the room in the darkness and slipped into bed with him. He felt her hand, light on his chest. She tugged his undershirt up and rested her hand on his stomach.

Miller rolled over to her and started to speak, but she cut him off.

"Don't say anything. Not now." Then she put her mouth on his.

He kept quiet, as she asked him to. And after the first time, she turned to him and he saw her smiling in the dark and he kissed her again. Then she slipped a leg over his and put her head on his chest. They were quiet again, not making any more sounds. Then she spoke.

"How old are you?"

Miller laughed. "Why are you asking that?"

"I don't care, or anything. I haven't been with an older guy before. I mean, you're what, forty?"

"Older than that."

"I'm twenty-five. The oldest guy I've dated was thirty-eight. But he was a punk. Not grown up, like you. He was a boy."

"We're both grown up."

"You know what I meant. Did you think this was some sort of kick for me?"

"It was something. Maybe we shouldn't think about it too much."

"It wasn't a kick," she said. "It wasn't just that. You just seem like a nice man, that's all. I feel comfortable with you. Is that strange?"

"No, it's not strange. I don't think. Thank you."

The girl laughed again. "God, maybe that's part of the attraction. You're so . . . formal. Maybe that's not the right word. Proper. No, that's not right either. You're polite, but I think you can be pretty mean when you want to be. Did you hurt that man? The one who insulted me?"

"Do you really want to know?"

"If you killed him or did something really bad to him, yes, I want to know."

Miller said, "I was a little rough with him. But he wasn't hurt. He didn't have to go to the hospital."

"How kind of you, not putting him in the hospital. What did he do to you?"

"He had me put in prison."

Sandra Slay took her hand off Miller's chest, held it off him briefly, and then set it back down.

"For what?" she said.

"For trafficking in narcotics. Not in this country. In Europe. I didn't do it. He framed me for it."

"Oh, God. Everyone I've ever met who's been in prison says they were set up."

"Did you believe them?"

"Almost never."

"That's good," Miller said. "You shouldn't."

"But I should believe you?"

Miller sighed and said, "That's up to you. I can try to persuade you I was framed. But what good would that do?"

"Well, I don't fancy being the kind of girl who sleeps with criminals. I'd like you to at least try to explain it."

"So you'll feel better?"

"Goddammit, Kurt. You don't have to be so shitty about it. If you're going to be like that—"

"I'm sorry," Miller said, interrupting. He faced her. "Really."

"I like you," she said. "There are not many men I like."

"Okay," Miller said. "Okay. What happened was I was an . . . I was a desk agent in Germany. An intelligence analyst working for the government. The man in the bar, he was working at the State Department at the time. He and another American came to Germany and tried to get me to change an intelligence report I wrote. They wanted me to change it because it got in the way

130

of their plans to launch a war in Syria. I told them I wouldn't do it and a couple of weeks later I was arrested in London. It was . . . it was easy for them to frame me because my brother is a criminal. A drug dealer. That cleared the way for them, because I was then discredited. And they got their war."

"You, one man, were in the way of them getting their war?"

"I didn't think you'd believe me. I have trouble believing it myself."

"That's not what I meant," the girl said. "I just don't—I just don't understand how one man or some report he wrote could get in the way of our country starting a war. I mean, this is America, man. When the people up top want to go to war, they just do it."

"Yes, generally."

"Yes, generally. But you don't believe this was a general situation?"

"I don't know," Miller said, sighing. He felt awkward, saying it out loud. It sounded more ridiculous when he gave voice to it. Maybe he had told her because of what they had shared.

Sandra said, "I vote, you know."

"Pardon?"

"I vote," she said. "I don't just sit back. I lost a brother in Iraq. He was killed by an IED bomb."

"Oh. I am sorry."

"He was on his third tour. We should have been outta there before he was killed. I voted for candidates who said they wanted to pull out of Iraq. But it didn't matter. I voted for the anti-war candidates and we ended up staying there anyway. It doesn't matter what the voters want. The people at the top just do whatever they want. Now they're talking about sending more troops back to Iraq."

"I'm sorry about your brother."

Miller heard her sigh in the dark. She seemed determined

131

not to weep about it. Maybe she was tapped out of grief.

"I don't know," she said. "You remind me of him in some ways. Sorry if that sounds kinky or . . . well, you know what I mean. He was a soldier. Which I kind of think you are. The way you carry yourself. He was very straight on, very proper. And very brave. A natural leader of men. And stubborn. Man, he was stubborn."

"Did he believe in it?"

"What do you mean, his mission?"

"Yes."

"Oh, yeah. He bought all of it. There were weapons of mass destruction. We were there to save the people of Iraq and promote democracy. He believed it all. He was one of those guys who believed everyone should serve in some capacity. If not in the military, then maybe as a cop or a firefighter. We're Dominican, you know. A lot of Dominicans take being a good American very seriously."

"You're from the West Indies?"

"That's where our parents came from. Don't tell me you didn't notice the cream in my coffee."

"Pardon?"

"Never mind. We're known as the Black Jews. Colin Powell, Sidney Poitier, even brother Malcolm X. All of them of West Indies background. You want to talk about discrimination, listen to a group of West Indians talk about American blacks. It's terrible."

"Maybe we're all tribal."

"That's a funny thing to say to a black girl you just made love to."

"I didn't really think about what color you are. Cream and coffee and such. Do you think Germans are like that?"

"I don't know."

"Boris Becker is married to a black woman."

"Who's Boris Becker?"

Miller smiled. "I don't know this Sein-feld, you don't know Becker. He was a tennis player. He won Wimbledon probably before you were born. He's Djokovic's coach now."

"How old is he?"

"He's about my age. You know, ancient."

"Are you teasing me?"

"No." Miller said, "I remember when he dominated Wimbledon in the eighties. The British press had headlines saying 'Blitzkreig' and other reminders of the war. And time and again, the British and American reporters would question him about the Second World War. This seventeen-year-old kid who was born about twenty years after it was all over. Like he had to somehow answer for it. I must say, he handled it remarkably well. Better than I would have."

"Did you play tennis?"

"Yes. I played a lot of sports. I was no champion."

"I said I thought you had been a soldier. Were you? Or do you mind me asking that?"

"I don't mind. Yes, I was a soldier. I've been to Afghanistan. And I've served with American soldiers."

"Are you sorry you did?"

"I don't spend much time revisiting the past. A German trait."

"You're being a smartass. Again."

"Yes, a little."

"You see my book?"

"Yes. You like Eric Hoffer?"

"It's okay. My brother gave it to me. Does that surprise you?"

"That you think Hoffer is okay or that your brother gave it to you?"

"Either."

"I suppose it's a coincidence. That you would be reading a book written by a German."

"No, I meant does it surprise you that a black girl would read a philosophy book."

Miller frowned. "What kind of question is that?"

"I don't know. Have you read Hoffer?"

"A long time ago. I saw him interviewed on television once. He was very loud and expressive. Too German for my tastes."

The girl laughed. "Funny to hear you say that."

"There are all kinds of Germans," Miller said. "We're not all like Bismarck, you know. Or that fat fellow who played *Goldfinger*. Or Hoffer."

"You know what? I think you're a bit of a snob."

"When it's called for."

Sandra said, "Hoffer wrote that people have a 'craving for pride.' He wrote that that was why the Vietnamese fought against the French and later the Americans. He didn't think it had much to do with communism."

"He was probably right about that."

"Do they talk about the war much in Germany?"

"What war?" Miller asked. Though he was pretty sure he knew.

"You know," she said. "About the Holocaust?"

"They do and they don't. The country guards against racism with laws even against speech. There are reminders everywhere of the past. Visual lessons. In Berlin, a memorial to the murdered Jews of Europe. Another of our museums is called the Topography of Terror and it's located at the old headquarters of the SS and the Gestapo. We rub our own face in it, so to speak. But no German likes Hitler jokes. My father told me when he was a boy, many people used to pray for Hitler. 'God keep and save the Fuehrer.' Even the swastika was a sort of twisted cross. My father was a religious man. He said the country was rife with that sort of blasphemy then."

"Are you a religious man?"

"No."

"This report you wrote, did you think it would prevent war?"

"No, I had no such illusions. Or vanity. When people want war, they'll always find a way to justify it. It's the way it's always been. But the men who came to see me, they somehow thought it was some sort of obstacle to what they wanted to do."

"You hate war?"

"Why would I not hate it?"

"I don't know. You're a soldier."

"Not many soldiers love war. The people who love it usually have never seen it up close."

"Have you seen it up close?"

"Yes."

"Is that why you wrote that report?"

"Oh, Christ. No. I wrote that report because it was the truth. You're not old enough to remember the wall coming down, are you?"

"The Berlin Wall?"

"Yes."

"No. I mean, I know what it was, if that's what you're asking. I am educated."

"I see that. Well, I remember it coming down. It seems silly now, but even back then, people feared the Germans. Feared what a united Germany would do. Even now, old-timers in England fear that Germany will form some sort of alliance with the Russian Bear and take over Europe. As if Russia were any sort of threat. But we're not like that. We care about money and beer and football. We have an army, but it's only for defense purposes. Perhaps because we're afraid of our own primitive impulses."

"And now?"

"We're still primitive. We're just a little more aware of it. Trust me, Germany still has its share of swine."

"You think we're primitive?"

"Who?"

"Americans."

"No, I don't think that. Twenty years ago, few people in the West feared America."

"Do you now?"

"Do I what now?"

"Fear the United States?"

After a moment, Miller said, "Sometimes. I'm not pro-American. I suppose you could say I'm anti-anti-American. I've usually found anti-Americans a tiresome lot. Too many of them are fools. Contemporary communists who still believe that Lenin and Mao were angels."

"What is your feeling about America now? Now that they've put you in prison?"

"I don't know," the German said in the dark. "What was done to me was done by a small group of people with a bad agenda. It wasn't done by your country."

"And now you've come here to settle the score."

He heard the patronizing tone in her voice. Miller said, "What's wrong with that?"

"I just think it's a bad idea, that's all. You're alive now and you're free. Isn't that enough?"

"No."

Sandra said, "Let me ask you something: Do you think it would make me feel any better if I somehow had the power to track down the men who killed my brother? If I could find them and kill them?"

"That is not the same."

"Why? Because he was killed in a war? Would it change things if I killed the men and women in Congress who authorized the war? Who whipped up the nation to a frenzy by making us all scared? What good would it do?"

"I can't answer that," Miller said. "I can only tell you I can't let these people get away with what they did to me."

"So it's about you."

"They came after me. I didn't start this."

"But you could walk away now. You could walk away and live."

"No, I think I've done too much at this stage for them to let me walk away."

"You say that as if you're glad. Glad that you forced them into this."

"I'm hardly glad about it."

"Satisfied then. You say you're a man of peace, but I wonder if some part of you welcomes this battle."

"They pay me what they owe me, there won't be any battle. It will be up to them."

"And if they don't?"

"I don't know," Miller said. "I'm too tired to think about that now. Are you sorry you invited me here?"

"I don't know yet." Sandra said, "Will you kiss me again?"

CHAPTER SEVENTEEN

Tanner told Hayes to follow the black girl for a couple of days to see if the German would turn up. Hayes agreed to do it because he was being paid to agree. But he doubted the German would come back to the black girl. Hayes didn't think the German would be dumb enough to do that. Hayes didn't even think the German would be in New York anymore. Tanner had said, "He's not as goddam clever as you think."

Tanner was still sore at Hayes. The way Tanner saw it, Hayes was responsible for failing to nail the kraut back at Bryant Park. Hayes had said, "The man never gave me the opportunity for a shot. You're the one who left."

But no, the almighty Tanner hadn't seen it that way. He said he had "improvised," the way any professional would have, and gone to the subway with the full intention of killing the German himself. Except the subway car had been crowded with too many people. Tanner would never admit the German may have outsmarted him.

Hayes was starting to think that Carl Tanner had been in management too long. All this emphasis on "planning." Shit, if you have the man in your sights on the subway, just plug him and be done with it. You shouldn't need the headset and the man in an apartment window waiting with a high-powered rifle.

So Hayes followed the black girl for a couple of days. From her apartment to her job at the bar and to some college where she was taking classes and then to some other bar where she worked. He wondered if he would die of boredom. He was a professional, not some private investigator waiting to see if someone was committing insurance fraud, jogging down the street when they're supposed to have a herniated disc. This job was beneath him.

But on the third day, he saw the black girl come out of the comedy club with a white man. The white man got on the back of her scooter with her and they took off.

It was dark and Hayes couldn't see the man too clearly. He was dressed nicely and he didn't look as young as the girl. But what did that mean? Hayes had never seen the German in person himself. He had only seen a file photo that could have been taken ten years earlier.

That was why Hayes didn't call Tanner and ask for backup. Tanner was back in Washington now and he would be angry as hell if Hayes brought him back here for nothing. *You called me because she was getting laid?* But Hayes was a hunter and he didn't mind sleeping in his car across the street from the girl's apartment to see if the man she had brought home was their target.

The girl lived on the second floor of a duplex in Brooklyn. It had a nice bay window at the front. After the sun came up, Hayes used the scope off his rifle and spent the better part of an hour sighting the window to see if the man would appear in front of it.

At around seven thirty a.m., the man did. The man came to the window dressed in jeans and a white T-shirt and Hayes slumped over in his seat to avoid being seen.

Hayes had only gotten a quick look at the man. But it was enough.

He decided to give the girl a half hour to leave. If she was still in her apartment he would kill them both. He hadn't received authorization to kill a bystander, but he would do it if the girl stayed too long. He had tailed the girl for a while now and had developed something of an attraction to her. She was a hot young thing with very nice skin and a great body. He wondered if he could get to know her if he didn't have to kill her.

But then with about five minutes left, Hayes saw the girl come out the front door of her apartment. He watched as she tucked her hair up and put her helmet on, watched as she got on her scooter and started it and rode away. Yeah, he thought. He would definitely have to drop by the bar where she worked, get to know her in private. Tonight would be good. He liked to reward himself with a girl after a job.

Hayes drove around the block and parked his car. He walked through a backyard over dead leaves and then came to the back of the duplex. He examined the back structure. There was an addition to the duplex that had been built to cover the back stairway. Probably about thirty years ago. That was good. Once he got in the back, neighbors would not be able to see him go up the steps. He would have to go through two doors. The first one to get to the stairwell. The second one to get into the girl's apartment. It shouldn't be hard. He had gone through doors before.

He jimmied the lock to the first door with a special card similar to a credit card, but stronger and more flexible. Then he was inside. Quietly, he closed the door behind him. He was then at the foot of the stairs. He heard the steady rhythm of a washing machine coming from the second floor. That was good. The noise would cover the sound of any creaking his footsteps would make. He climbed the stairs. He stopped on the landing between the stairs and hesitated for a moment. He pulled his semiautomatic pistol from his pocket and fixed the silencer to the barrel. Then he walked up the second landing.

He stopped near the last step. Now he could see the washing

machine. Now he heard its thrum. He looked at the door into the second-floor apartment. If the girl was using the machine, odds were she had left that door unlocked. Hayes went to the door and slowly twisted the knob. The door was unlocked. When the knob was fully turned, he pushed the door open.

Now he could see into the apartment. He stepped into the kitchen. On the counter was a coffee pot, half full, the red light on, the coffee hot. In front of him was a marble counter. To his right, a kitchen table in front of the refrigerator. At the table there was a jacket draped over one of the chairs. There was no one in the kitchen.

Beyond the kitchen was a hallway. On the left side was a closed door. And now Hayes could hear the shower running. On the right side was another closed door. Hayes looked at both doors and determined which one was the bedroom and which one was the bathroom. The shower sound was coming from the closed door on the left. The last time he had seen the German was in the front of the apartment. That would be the living room. The German had been dressed when Hayes saw him through the window. Hayes crept forward and went to the front of the bathroom door. He put his hand on the doorknob.

"Drop the gun please."

Hayes froze. *Christ.* The German was behind him. He must have been in the kitchen. Hiding . . . where? Christ, behind that marble counter. It would have been the only place he could have hidden. Hayes had walked right past him.

Hayes had his gun raised, close to his chest. He did not turn to see the voice behind him. Hayes said, "Are you armed?"

It seemed a reasonable question.

Miller said, "What do you think?"

He was a cool one, Hayes thought. But maybe he was full of shit. Hayes whirled around and the first shot caught him above the rib cage. Hayes began to sink and Miller pulled the trigger of his revolver again and then again and hit Hayes in the chest with both shots. Hayes dropped to the floor.

Hayes lost his gun in the fall. He saw it near his left hand as the German came toward him. Hayes reached out for the pistol and Miller stepped on his wrist.

Hayes looked up at the German. He was smaller than Hayes had thought him to be. The German standing there in a blue bathrobe. The German now holding his revolver with two hands, the barrel aimed at Hayes's face.

Hayes struggled to breath, his chest making sucking sounds. Hayes thinking it was the first shot that probably went under his armpit and tumbled into his heart. If that was what happened, it wouldn't be long. Hayes knew he was going into shock. The German seemed to look at him with a sad expression.

Hayes said, "I had . . . to . . . I had to find out."

"And you did," Miller said. "Tanner send you?"

Hayes nodded. He said, "Were you behind the counter?"

"Yes. I heard you at the door."

"Christ," Hayes said. "I should have known."

"You shouldn't have tried to come in. Are there others?" Miller stepped harder on his wrist. "Answer me. Are there others?"

Hayes moaned. "No! . . . no . . . Not here. But there are others."

"Where? Where are they?"

"The shower," Hayes said. "Why . . . ?"

"I was waiting in the kitchen while the water got hot," Miller said. "Where are the others?"

But Hayes was dead.

CHAPTER EIGHTEEN

Tanner said, "He left him at Port Authority. He was on a bench with newspapers covering him like a blanket. Like a hobo. A transit cop came along and told him to move. He moved the newspapers and saw that he was dead. Shot three times."

Gehlen said, "How do you know it was the German? How do you know the German killed him?"

"Oh for Christ's sake," Tanner said. "Of course it was the German. The man killed Hayes and put his corpse at one of the most public places he could think of. It was the same thing he did with Carson. He wanted Hayes to be found."

"Why would he do that?"

"Because he wants us to know about it," Tanner said. "He could have dumped his body in the river or any number of places. He wanted us to know he killed Hayes."

"Why did Hayes go after him by himself?"

"Because he was stupid," Tanner said.

They were in Gehlen's office in Washington. It was a nice office with a view of the Capitol dome. Outside tourists in tennis shoes trudged through damp cold, determined to see every part of the Smithsonian.

Gehlen said, "Maybe Hayes underestimated him."

"Maybe."

Gehlen said, "Or maybe you did."

Tanner sighed. "I didn't underestimate him. He was a desk analyst. A foreigner."

"It seems to me," Gehlen said, "that this man is something more than an analyst. It seems he had some sort of military training. Maybe something more than that. Was he a soldier of some sort?"

"I don't know."

"Well, don't you think that's something you should have looked into before you targeted him?"

Tanner said, "I targeted him at your direction. You sent me to Germany to talk him into amending his report. When he wouldn't do it, you told me to take him out of the equation. I did what you told me to do."

"But you left him alive."

"You didn't want him dead then."

"Well things have changed now. Before he was a nuisance. An obstacle. Now he's an enemy of the State. A terrorist killing Americans on American soil."

Tanner said, "Okay, then. Do you want to alert the FBI? The NYPD? They can find him."

"If they do, they'll arrest him," Gehlen said. "We don't want him arrested. The last thing we need is some sort of public trial where he can start naming names. Your name, my name, Lindsey's name. We can't have that. His sentence has already been determined."

"And that sentence is death?"

"Didn't I say that?"

"I wanted to hear it from you."

"You've heard it. Now get it done."

"Okay."

"You say okay, but the man is still out there. You understand what's at stake here?"

"Remind me."

Gehlen didn't pick up the mild disdain in Tanner's tone. Gehlen said, "The future of freedom. It's worth a bit of blood to keep this country secure. If called for, more than a bit. This man gets arrested, he'll have a trial. There are people in this country who will demand it. They will say that it's un-American not to give this terrorist due process. They don't understand what sort of world we live in. They don't understand the reality, the danger. Freedom has to be protected. It's not a question of whether or not we should use secret police or action teams who use deadly force. We don't have a choice."

Christ, Tanner thought. Gehlen making speeches again. Like he was on *Meet the Press*. It wasn't necessary.

"I got it," Tanner said. "We won't call the FBI then. But we don't have an unlimited supply of men. You and Madam Horvath have assigned a lot of my crew to spying on other candidates and political enemies to find out their secrets and vulnerabilities. They're scattered all over the country, peeking in hotel windows and collecting incriminating videotapes and photos and threatening the occasional precinct local. They can continue with that work. Or they can look for Kurt Miller. But they can't do both."

"Then you pull them off those details until this is done."

"You're the boss," Tanner said. "But are you certain Miller rates this high a priority?"

"I've just told you he does. What, are you afraid of him now?"

Carl Tanner sighed. Jay Gehlen had probably never even held a gun in his hand. The Gehlens of this world always farmed out the dirty work to people like Tanner. But man, they loved to talk tough.

"No, Jay, I'm not afraid of him. I look at things practically. Rationally."

"And what, in your opinion, constitutes the practical, rational choice?"

"One rational alternative is that we pay him," Tanner said.

Gehlen stared at Tanner for a while.

"Pay him," Gehlen said.

"Give him what he's asking for and let him go home and forget about him."

"Pay him a million dollars."

"A million dollars isn't exactly a lot of money these days," Tanner said. "Lindsey can make it back in about five speaking engagements. We've given more money than that to murderous sheiks in Afghanistan. We don't have to like them to pay them off."

"I see," Gehlen said. "He kills one man and now you're afraid he'll kill you. Is that it?"

"He gets within a mile of me, he's a dead man. *I'm* not worried about him."

"So I should be?"

After a moment, Tanner said, "Maybe. He knows who you are. He knows Lindsey was behind this."

"You think he'd kill a Presidential candidate?"

"If he thought she was trying to kill him, he might." Tanner said, "In his mind, it might constitute self-defense."

Jay Gehlen was quiet for a few moments. He had not considered the possibility that the German could do something like that. The German was a product of a civilized western country. A former intelligence agent. . . . Surely not? No, Tanner was trying to sell him something he probably didn't believe himself.

Gehlen said, "I don't think that's a likely possibility."

"That's what the Kennedys thought too," Tanner said. "They tried to have Castro assassinated. They tried pretty hard and failed. And then Kennedy was killed by a Marxist in Dallas. Maybe it was tied to Castro, maybe it wasn't. My point is, Jay, when you get into this business of assassination, you should understand the risks."

"All right," Gehlen said, "you've explained the risks. And

you've convinced me you're not afraid of the man. But I'm not going back to Lindsey and asking her to give a million dollars to a terrorist. You find that fiend and put him down. Is that understood?"

Tanner nodded. "So we're not contacting the FBI or Secret Service?"

"Didn't I just tell you we weren't?"

Tanner suppressed a smile. "You did. I just didn't want there to be any misunderstanding on that point."

CHAPTER NINETEEN

The children of the Latimer County Praise Orchestra sang Lee Greenwood's "God Bless the U.S.A." like it was a hymn. The audience sung along with them. A banner hung across the stage reading *Saving America*. When the song was done, a slender woman of about fifty came to the podium and gave a speech about the importance of including the phrase "Under God" in the Pledge of Allegiance. She then inferred, without evidence, that the current occupant of the White House had a secret plan to remove the words from the Pledge. Then she offered a prayer to "put people in" public office who would "do the right thing" and for people in America to "rise up" to confront the evil of their times. She closed with a quote from Romans. Then she introduced the woman who was going to save their country.

There was a standing ovation as Lindsey Horvath came to the podium. Lindsey let them cheer as she took her time surveying the masses. She pointed at a minor party official in the crowd, widened her eyes in surprise, and smiled a "Hey, it's you!" She did this even though she had been talking to the man an hour earlier. A crowd-pleasing move she had honed over the years. Then she began to speak.

She told them she was glad to be with the *real* people of Virginia where "sushi is still called by its proper name: bait." That got a laugh along with a little poke at the Liberals dominating the northern part of the state. She took the flattery in and eased into a more serious tone and said that before she got started, she wanted the State of Virginia to take a moment to acknowledge her good friend Staff Sergeant Shep Luckowski. The crowd murmured a bit in confusion and looked around till their eyes settled on a uniformed soldier who stood with the assistance of crutches. He had lost one of his legs in Syria. Lindsey exploited the pause before the cheers began and got in that "Men like Shep Luckowski are the real heroes of this nation. They are protecting our freedoms!" The young soldier nodded uneasily as the crowd gave him a standing ovation. He looked around, somewhat bewildered, as Lindsey Horvath herself clapped her gratitude to him.

Later in the speech, Lindsey said, "Unlike our brave soldiers, there are people in Washington who don't want to do what's necessary to thwart the threat of terrorism. They counsel caution and speak of measured risks. They say, 'We're not the world's policeman.' They say that the American people have grown tired and weary of war. They come up with excuse after excuse to justify sticking their heads in the sand. Well, I say, let them come to Latimer County and explain to us why they can't get the job done. The people of Virginia know that excuses are like rear ends: everyone's got one and they all stink."

After the applause and laughter receded, she put a little southern twang in her tone and said, "Let 'em come here and tell us that freedom is free. That the sacrifices our soldiers have made were in vain. Let them try to tell us we don't understand the peril this country is in. If we don't fight the enemy in Syria and Iraq and Iran, we'll be fighting them here. What is provocative in the world is not American strength. What is provocative is American weakness."

A mild cheer then, which was okay with Lindsey. She was only looking for a short pause in the pace. It was like conducting an orchestra.

"The problem is not that we're doing too much. It's that

we're doing too little. We are not committed to victory. We are not committed to greatness. There is a tide of moral relativism and lack of will that is poisoning this great country from within. We've defeated the Soviet Union only to have some in Washington tell us that we should treat terrorists the same way we treat armed robbers. We've pushed the communists out the front door only to let the terrorists come in the back. The liberals say, give them trials and lawyers and let them clog up our courts. You know, the way we do for drug dealers and murderers. Treat terrorism as if it's just another crime.

"These are not the actions of a country serious about the threat to America. The enemy watches and sees that we are weak and unsure. They see that we have forgotten what we are about, who we are as a people.

"But now is not the time to give in to cynical defeatism. Now is not the time to lower the flag. Not on my watch!"

A roar from the crowd.

Lindsey's eyes shone as she said, "You know and I know that accepting defeat is not what America is about. I believe that we need to return to the basics. A return to values. A return to biblical morality. This is not only the right thing to do, it is the smart thing to do. It is a matter of survival. For the terrorists know that when we are morally weak, we have lost our will to fight. The alternative is instability and the corruption of our very souls. We cannot ignore evil. We cannot close the door and hope that it will simply go away. It won't. Like a minister of God, we have a duty to execute wrath upon those who do evil.

"We have to be forward deployed. We cannot go back. When we deploy forward, people see us for what we are. They see our power. They see our compassion. They see our resolve. And, best of all, they see our patriotism. And they say, *there*. There's a country we want to be on board with."

★ ★ ★ ★ ★

Lindsey's next stop was an ice cream plant outside Richmond. She did not give a speech there, but went out on the floor to shake hands with workers wearing hair nets. The plant manager was polite to her, but only just. He was a military veteran, jaded by the experience and immune to the empty charm of celebrity. Lindsey asked a couple of questions about how the ice cream was made and the foreperson decided to pretend her interest was genuine. Later, she asked the plant manager if there was a private room she could use to check her e-mails and rest for a while. The plant manager led her up a set of iron steps to his office, which overlooked the plant floor.

Lindsey posted her bodyguard outside the office and went inside. There was a large rectangular window overlooking the operations. Lindsey closed the door and lowered the blinds on the window. She took her iPad out of her satchel and opened it up. She opened the e-mail from her husband. He said he was back in Washington and their son was doing well at Choate and he had made the hockey team. She scrolled down to the e-mail from Meena, her aide. That one she responded to, saying she missed her too and that she should be back in Washington tonight.

The bodyguard outside the door was a former FBI agent named Mel Lightman. He was standard-fed fare. Tall and broad shouldered and wearing a Jos. A. Bank suit. He carried a Magnum pistol in a harness under his suit and he was very sure of himself. When a worker in a hair net approached him and asked if he could speak with Mr. Davis, the plant manager, Lightman told him Mr. Davis was either out on the plant floor or in the break room. Lightman pointed toward the stairway as if to direct the ice cream maker away.

"Excuse me?" the worker said.

"Beat it," Lightman said.

"Yes, sir," the worker said.

Lightman made the mistake of briefly turning his back on the worker. Lightman felt his knee buckle as the worker kicked him behind the knee and as he sank to the ground he felt a strong arm encircle his neck and a damp chloroformed cloth clamped over his mouth and nose. He struggled and tried to cry out but the German's grip was strong and soon the former FBI man lost consciousness.

Miller dragged him into the bathroom. He bound the bodyguard's feet and hands and gagged his mouth. He left the bodyguard in a stall with the door locked from the inside.

Miller went into the plant manager's office and closed the door behind him. He pulled the hair net off and tossed it onto a couch.

Lindsey Horvath was still sitting at the plant manager's desk typing on her iPad. She looked up and saw what she thought was a blue-collar clock-puncher.

"What do you want?"

Miller said, "I thought we should talk."

"Come back when your boss is here," she said. "I'm very busy." She waved her hand in dismissal.

Miller stood there.

"Seriously," Lindsey said. "Get out."

Miller said, "But we haven't talked yet."

"I have nothing to—"

Lindsey stopped and looked again at the man. He was wearing jeans and a T-shirt, but not the sort of denim shirt or Dickie work pants she had seen on the other employees. He was not wearing a coat or a jacket. Nothing to hide a gun in. Still . . .

Lindsey said, "How did you get in here?"

"Your man is in the bathroom," Miller said. "I think he's going to be there for a while."

Lindsey started to reach into her bag for her cell phone.

"No, don't do that," Miller said. "Put your hands on the desk, please. Go on."

Lindsey hesitated, but put her hands on the desk. Then, in what Miller thought was an impressive gesture, she closed the iPad. It put her up a notch. She was a cool one, Miller thought. Formidable indeed and not to be underestimated.

Lindsey said, "You're the German, aren't you?"

"Yes."

She studied him for a long moment.

Then she said, "Well, what do you want? Did you come here to talk or did you come here to kill me?"

Yes, quite formidable.

"Nothing so dramatic," Miller said. "I came here to speak to you to see if we could come to an agreement. To see if we could avoid any further conflict." Miller took a seat in front of the desk.

Lindsey said, "What sort of conflict would I have with you?"

"One of Mr. Tanner's men tried to kill me. You know about that, uh."

"I know about it. You killed that man."

"In self-defense, Miss. I am not a murderer."

"You killed an American on American soil," Lindsey said. "I don't think your theory of self-defense is going to go very far."

"Perhaps. But we are not in court."

"No," Lindsey said, "we're at an ice cream plant in Shitville, Virginia. You ever run for public office?"

Miller shook his head.

"No, of course you haven't. You're a desk man, aren't you? Another underpaid civil servant taking home a check every two weeks. You wouldn't understand what this is about."

"Enlighten me."

"It's eighteen-hour days of shaking hands and smiling at fools and currying favor with the local precinct captains. It takes discipline to do that. It takes strength. Mental strength, not just the sort of physical strength you would use to dump some bodyguard into a toilet. Or kill a man in New York."

"I didn't start the killing. I would not have had to do anything if you had paid me what you owe me."

Lindsey Horvath looked at him again. "What I owe you. Is that how you see this?"

"You approved the operation to put me in jail. You took something from me so you could have your war. Okay, you got your war. But I no longer have my livelihood. Or my pension."

"You want to be compensated, is that it?"

"Yes."

"Or what?"

"Or I tell people that you had Paul Posner murdered."

Lindsey smiled and shook her head. "You think I ordered that?"

"I do."

"You think you can prove that?"

"Maybe."

"If you think that, why don't you go to the police and tell them? Why don't you report it to the FBI? Get your just result that way."

Miller said nothing.

Lindsey said, "Shall I answer that question for you? You won't because you know nobody will believe you. They'll say you're just another European conspiracy theorist. You could just as well tell them I planned the 9/11 attacks."

"Perhaps," Miller said. "But if your man Tanner is arrested for the murder of Posner, he won't go down for it by himself. Not for you or for Mr. Gehlen. He'll take steps to protect himself. He'll name names, as the Americans say."

Lindsey Horvath opened her mouth and closed it. For the first time, Miller saw a crack in her composure.

Miller said, "Surely, you've considered that, haven't you?"

Lindsey quickly regained herself. "Oh, that's clever. That's cute. Are you telling me Tanner admitted this to you?"

"Oh, he was remarkably frank about it. But if you don't believe he told me, ask him yourself."

"I don't believe you. But even if I did, Tanner's not going to do anything to endanger my career. He's a team player."

"No, what he is is a mercenary. Believe me, I know the type. And team players tend to disperse after criminal charges have been filed. For every Richard Nixon, there is a John Dean willing to turn state's evidence."

Lindsey Horvath smiled. "Ah, so you know something about American history? That's very impressive. You met Paul Posner, did you?"

"Yes."

"What did you think of him?"

"I thought he was a good man."

"Yeah, I suppose you would. Now don't take this as some sort of admission on my part, but Posner was weak. He was indecisive. These are not the times for indecisive men."

"So you did have him killed."

"I didn't say that," Lindsey said. She smiled again, pleased with her clever non-admission admission.

"But you want me to know you ordered it all the same," Miller said. He suddenly felt a disgust and weariness he had not expected. A withering under the brace of this woman's chilly smile.

Miller said, "You are of the political class, uh?"

"If you say so."

"But of course you've never seen war up close."

"I've been in the war room, Mr. Miller."

"You've watched images on a screen, no doubt. But you haven't *seen* war. A friend of mine was killed in Afghanistan recently. He was an American. I'd tell you his name but you wouldn't know it. Or care. You see, he's not able to stand up at one of your rallies."

"If he was an American, he died fighting for something good. Sacrifices have to be made."

"But not by people like you," Miller said. "I heard your speech back there in Latimer County. Yes, I was there. You said something about 'American weakness being provocative.' That sort of bunkum may please the locals, but it's not going to impress a mercenary like Tanner if he's facing a lifetime in the penitentiary."

"You call it bunkum," Lindsey said. "You lecture me about rousing the local populace. You, a German, lecture me about war and peace and crowds of people blindly following along. You Germans, you're extreme in your savagery and a few decades later you have the gall to be extreme in your pacifism. You never consider the middle ground. And now you look at me and figure I'm just another crass, political opportunist. But you don't know me at all. You don't know what I'm about or who I am."

"And what is that?"

Lindsey leaned forward. "A woman who believes in her country. Her people. A woman who believes in freedom and America's place in the world."

Miller sighed and said, "Well, I'm not sure I understand what you mean when you talk about freedom. And I still haven't figured out what it means to be 'forward deployed.' Freedom . . . the freedom to do what? To bomb people in other countries, perhaps? To torture captives and disregard the Geneva Convention? To put people you know to be innocent in prison? And then send assassins after them? You do these things and then point to the history of the Third Reich and say, 'Nothing we've done is as bad as that.' And so far, you are correct. We have provided you a measuring stick of horror and brutality even you cannot match."

"Americans are not Nazis," Lindsey said.

"Anyone can be a Nazi, Ms. Horvath, given the opportunity and the means. All the discussion of the Holocaust and trials of Nuremberg did nothing to prevent Pol Pot and Mao from slaughtering their millions. It did nothing to stop your government from raining bombs on Vietnamese civilians who mostly just wished to be left alone. That vicious, reptilian capacity is in all of us. But you are right to be skeptical about Germans preaching pacifism. Maybe even cynical. We allowed ourselves to be seduced by a demon preaching fear and hatred. We put order and glory before the individual and even God. And indeed, as you say, we blindly followed along. Like you, Hitler romanticized war. Death and destruction were things of beauty to him. Works of art. But naive though it may be, I like to think the Germans won't make that mistake again. All the romantic notions of war and blood and glory have been pounded out of us. Reduced to rubble in Dresden and Berlin. I suppose we have the Americans to thank for bringing us to our senses. . . . Ah, but what am I talking about? All your talk of freedom and forward deployment, it's a lot of shit. All you're interested in is power. You killed Posner and I'm going to make sure people know about it."

Miller stood.

Lindsey said, "What about your money?"

Miller said, "I don't want it anymore."

CHAPTER TWENTY

It was about midnight when Gehlen got to Lindsey's townhouse in Georgetown. The security detail had now been doubled. Three of Tanner's men guarding the front and two more in the back.

Lindsey's assistant, Meena Katkar, let him in the front door. Meena looked up and down the street before letting Gehlen in and Gehlen had to stop himself from rolling his eyes. It wasn't a good idea to piss off Meena.

Meena was about a year shy of thirty. She was full in the hips and heavy breasted and had flawless skin. She was a first-generation American with an East-Indian background. She was raised a Catholic and made a point of telling people she was a devout Christian. She had a husband back in California, though Gehlen had only met him once. She had been working for Lindsey since she was a college student.

Meena said, "She's ready for you."

Gehlen swallowed some more resentment and pride. This kid he had met when she was a twenty-one-year-old intern now letting him know she controlled "access" or something. Parasite. She wasn't even that smart. Though Gehlen had long suspected that intelligence was not what had drawn Lindsey to her.

Meena escorted Gehlen into the living room. A gas fire lit up the fireplace. Lindsey paced up and down in front of it as she talked on the phone.

"No," Lindsey said, "you tell him he is not to speak to anyone about it. He's being paid to keep his mouth shut. . . . Yes, we'll continue to pay him in the interim. And if I get word that the police have been called, I will get evil. Do you understand? . . . Good."

Lindsey dropped the cell phone in to the pocket of her silk bathrobe. She looked at Gehlen and then at her aide.

"Meena, go wait in the bedroom."

Meena gave them their privacy and Lindsey said, "He came to me today."

"Who?"

"Your German. Miller."

Gehlen paled and took a seat. "Christ. How?"

"He snuck into the ice cream plant and knocked out that idiot security guard I had."

"Who was working security?"

"I don't know. . . . His name was Lightman."

"Not one of Tanner's people."

"Oh fuck, Jay. What difference does it make? Tanner's men or some off-duty jackoff from the FBI. He let security be breached."

"How bad?"

"Bad. The German was close enough to me to touch me. He had me alone for almost fifteen minutes."

"Are you sure it was him?"

"Yes. The things he said, the things he knew. It was him."

Gehlen looked at his boss again. Standing there in her dressing gown. No makeup and her hair pulled back. An unflattering appearance, which didn't bother her. More to the point, she didn't seem frightened. She just seemed angry.

Gehlen said, "Are you all right?"

"I'm standing here, aren't I?"

"Yes, I see that. But . . . he didn't hurt you?"

"No. He just threatened me." Lindsey sighed and said, "I

think we've got it under control. It shouldn't get out."

"Excuse me?"

"No one knows he was there," Lindsey said. "Lightman was chloroformed or something. I had him taken to the hospital. He's okay. I told him that whoever did that to him never got near me. He agreed not to report it."

"You didn't report it?"

"No." She looked at Gehlen curiously. "Why would I?"

"You said he threatened you."

"Yeah. He said if I didn't pay him his money, he'd kill me. Oh, and now he wants two million."

"Two million?"

"Yeah. He's getting angrier because we haven't paid him."

"Oh, man," Gehlen said. He was suddenly very tired. "Maybe . . ."

"Maybe what, Jay? Don't you dare tell me that maybe we should contact the Secret Service and tell them about this."

"I—I only think that we should consider it. If he got close enough to you to hurt you."

"You think I'm afraid of him?"

"Shouldn't you be?"

"Jay, a commander in chief has to deal with such things. I've been shot at by snipers before. It didn't rattle me then. And I'm not rattled now."

Gehlen bit his lip. The infamous Sierra Leone sniper story. Lindsey claimed she had been shot at by anti-American rebels in Africa during a goodwill tour. No witnesses could be found to corroborate the story. Gehlen had advised her long ago not to talk about Sierra Leone anymore as it made her "vulnerable" to political enemies. So far, she had taken his advice. Maybe it was okay if she just told the story in private.

"All right," Gehlen said. "We don't tell Secret Service how close Miller got to you. Or even about his existence. But you have to request their protection."

"*You're* supposed to protect me. You and your man Tanner. What am I paying him all this money for? Miller was close enough to me to kill me. Where were your people?"

"You said you didn't want—"

"Never mind what I said."

"Yes, ma'am. We've already increased security around you. It won't happen again."

"It better not."

Lindsey took a seat and folded her legs. She sighed and said, "Jay."

"Yes, ma'am."

"What do you know about Tanner?"

"He's reliable. He'll do whatever we tell him."

"No, I don't mean that. I mean, what do you think he'd do if he were questioned about Posner?"

Gehlen shifted in his seat. "I don't think anyone is going to question him about that."

"But what if they do?"

"It's . . . not going to come to that. No one knows anything about it. It happened so long ago."

"It wasn't that long ago. There's no statute of limitations on murder."

"That case has been closed."

"What if it were reopened?"

"I just don't see how that could happen. The case was resolved. Someone robbed a liquor store and killed a clerk and a witness. Case closed."

"Is there a way we could get someone else to confess to it?"

"Oh . . . I think that would be very difficult."

"Let's say, hypothetically, Tanner was questioned about it. Can we trust him to protect us?"

Gehlen was uncomfortable with the word *us*. He said,

"Tanner's not going to be questioned by anyone. Why are you concerned about this now?"

"I just don't like loose ends."

"I don't either, but . . . wait, did Miller bring this up to you?"

"Yes."

"He brought up Posner's murder?"

"Yes. He told me he thinks I had it done."

After a moment, Gehlen said, "What did you say?"

"I told him he was crazy."

"Is that why he wants two million now? He's threatened blackmail over Posner?"

"Right."

"But I thought you said he threatened to kill you?"

"Yes, he did that too."

But if he had threatened to kill her, Gehlen thought, *why wasn't she scared?* Few people can receive a death threat up close and not be fazed by it.

"Well," Gehlen said, "which is it? He said he'd kill you if you didn't pay him? Or he said he'd expose you for having Posner killed if you didn't pay him?"

"He said both things. Goddammit, Jay, aren't you listening?"

"Yes, ma'am."

"Look, the man is insane. He has to be stopped. I don't want him found by the Secret Service. I don't want him arrested. He needs to be located and terminated before he leaves the country."

"He's leaving the country?"

"Well, he might."

"Then how could he try to kill you if he's leaving?"

"Christ! Why are you asking all these questions? I don't know. I told you, he's crazy. He's a terrorist. They're not rational. Will you for chrissakes get this done?"

★ ★ ★ ★ ★

After Gehlen left, Lindsey went to the bedroom. Meena was in the bed reading *Major Pettigrew's Last Stand*. Meena was in her pajamas now. She looked up from her book and said, "How did it go?"

"Fine," Lindsey said. "He left here with his tail between his legs. Faggot."

Meena said, "Would you like some tea?"

"No, I don't want any fucking tea." She looked at Meena and here expression softened a bit. "Sorry."

"It's all right." Meena extended her hand. "Come to bed."

CHAPTER TWENTY-ONE

In another part of Washington, Miller sat at a hotel bar nursing his second beer. The television behind the bar was turned to ESPN, a couple of guys arguing about the new college football playoff system. A tall, bald guy saying, "I thought this would be better. It's actually worse." Miller could see they took college football very seriously here. Not being American, he didn't understand its appeal. He thought the game had too many fits and starts. It lacked the flow and beauty of European football.

He remembered when Germany had hosted the World Cup. The Germans so well behaved. It was the English fans the police worried about. All those violent hooligans. Even the Germans found it odd that they were now the ones in fear of the English. Of course, the German police didn't worry about the American fans at all. They were so clean and polite. German waitresses liked serving them because they were such generous tippers.

How could a country with people like that produce a woman like Lindsey Horvath? A woman so filled with bile. What had made her so angry? So determined? Surely, she hadn't been abused as a child. She had grown up with advantages and wealth. Yet here she was.

Miller knew he was at something of a disadvantage with people like this. The terrorist he could usually understand. They were more often than not losers, trying to seek identity through violence and religion and unworthy causes. Some he had interviewed seemed almost adolescent in their stubbornly held

164

views. Islamists, skinheads, militant leftists. He had dealt with them all. He had handled them with professional detachment and got them to reveal things about their crimes and their comrades and then he had tried to put them behind bars for as long as the law would permit. He felt little sympathy for them. On the whole, they were brutal and unregenerate.

But Lindsey Horvath was different. Lindsey Horvath was attached to some sort of . . . *power* he had not yet encountered.

One of Miller's favorite American films from his childhood had a scene where the hero says, "I'm only scared of two things: women and the police." Miller had not spent much of his life in fear of women. But Lindsey Horvath scared him.

He wanted to dismiss her as another political clown. There had been American fascists before her and they had never been able to do too much damage. Their McCarthy had drunk himself out of relevance. And FDR had successfully marginalized old Joe Kennedy when he fully came to understand the extent of the man's hatred for Jews. And the good-looking, steel-hearted woman from Alaska seemed more interested in being a celebrity than a politician. The hardcore haters never seemed to get too far in American politics. The U.S. had never really been helmed by a genuine monster. America, for all its faults, had never produced a Hitler or a Lenin or a Stalin. It had produced Eisenhowers and Washingtons and Lincolns. Maybe it *had* been a blessed nation. Maybe it was exceptional. Or maybe it was their system that was exceptional. The checks and balances supplied by the legislature and the judiciary that prevented any man or woman from having too much power. Prevented them from having their enemies shot.

But Lindsey Horvath had admitted to him that she had a man shot. An American, no less.

For what? What had Paul Posner done that merited his murder?

He had told Miller that he believed Miller's report was sound. Maybe he intended to defend the validity of Miller's report once he was back in the States. But, no, that wouldn't make any sense. The President himself had read that report.

So it had to be something more. Maybe Horvath's men had tried to lean on Posner and get him to denounce the report too. And maybe, possibly, Posner had figured out what they had done to Miller. That they had framed him for a crime. Maybe Posner had threatened to make *that* public. Or maybe Posner had threatened them because of some other crime they had committed.

Miller believed he would never find out the real reason they killed Posner. Tanner or Gehlen would never tell him. And though Lindsey Horvath almost bragged of having given the order, she would probably never admit to him her reasons for doing it. She was too smart for that.

How smart was she? Smart enough to turn a democracy into a dictatorship? It had taken Hitler only five months to destroy German democracy after he came to power. In that time, he had pushed his Emergency Decree through what was left of the German government in the name of the "Protection of the People and the State." German legislators surrounded by SA thugs voted in favor of it. Some of them supported it out of fear, but plenty of others supported it because they thought it was good for Germany. The decree enabled the state police to bypass the courts completely. It eliminated freedom of the press. It gave all power to the Fuehrer. And after the decree went into effect, people who didn't like Nazis simply disappeared. There was no law left to protect them. The most cultured nation in Europe became a genuine terrorist state.

Surely, Lindsey Horvath could not pull off something like that. And if she couldn't, why should Miller be afraid of her? Even if he had some way of truly knowing she had that sort of capability, he couldn't just kill her. It would make him a murderer. A lunatic. And even if he put her down, she might be replaced by some other demagogue within a matter of weeks. Some other demagogue speaking of God's will and wanting to make America an empire instead of a republic. Would you kill that one too?

Christ, Miller thought. Nobody ever learns. They fall for the empty promise and glory of empire until they try to extend one and get their asses handed to them. He had stood and watched the woman speak about religious destiny and knew without question she had about as much religious conviction as an IRA gangster. Empire was the true god of people like Lindsey Horvath. An Imperial United States of America was her holy ghost.

Well . . . it was her country and if the Americans wanted her for a leader, good luck to them. It wasn't his duty to protect America from itself. Still, he wondered why any intelligent American would want an empire. Why would they risk peace and prosperity to attain it? It didn't make any country more safe or secure. It did the opposite, in fact. The British Empire may have done India some good, but it didn't do much for Britain other than to bankrupt her and leave her vulnerable to the Germans. And Hitler and the Kaiser's dreams of an Imperial Germany just reduced it to rubble. France's ambitions to maintain an empire had led them to try to hold on to Indochina and that led to the humiliation of Dien Bien Phu and the mess that was the Vietnam War. To Miller, empire-building was just an extension of vanity, and a costly one at that.

And what about you? Miller thought. He had followed Horvath with the full intention of getting money from her. He felt he deserved it after what she had done to him. But then he had seen the way she had moved the masses, saw the rabid gleam in her eyes, and he began to doubt himself. He wondered if he started to fear her then. Or maybe it wasn't fear. Maybe it was just disgust. That he should contemplate taking money off such a person. That he should accept payment from her. That he should accept a payoff from someone who could smile at him while she admitted she had ordered the death of a man. You were going to take money from her, Miller thought. *What does that say about you?*

So he hadn't taken the money. But Paul Posner was still dead, along with some poor clerk at a liquor store. They had killed American citizens in a Washington suburb without any hesitation. And now Lindsey Horvath would have him killed too. So . . . he had good reason to fear her.

Miller thought of his brother Manfred. Manfred liked to say, "We're all whores." Manfred defending his flesh trade. If Manfred knew Miller had changed his mind about the money, he would probably shake his head in wonder. *You go all the way to America to get payment and then you decide you don't want it. No wonder you didn't go into business.*

But no, Manfred wouldn't say that. Manfred and Bruno Barzen would have both told him to stay in Europe and stay away from the States. Whether he was chasing revenge or a payoff, it was a bad idea.

He could go home now. Go back to Germany and forget about this. But, as he had told Sandra Slay, he had done too much to go back. Tanner or someone working for him would come to Germany and kill him. He'd killed one of Tanner's men. He had gotten close enough to Lindsey Horvath to touch her. They weren't going to forget about that. He could die here soon or die in Germany later.

Miller was inside the Beltway now. Just a few miles from the Capitol. He could drive there in the morning and . . . and do what? Ask if he can testify at some sort of congressional hearing? Ask if he could speak to the President?

He smiled at the thought and wondered if he was losing his

sanity. Yes, go to the President and explain to him why he should take the word of a convicted criminal. Better yet, go to the FBI, as Lindsey Horvath had suggested. Taunting him. Reminding him of his powerlessness and lack of credibility. Go to the FBI and see if they write a report before they locked him up.

The FBI.

It triggered something. The FBI Annual Report . . . two years ago. A memorandum he'd written after doing his review of the FBI Annual Report. A memorandum he had been asked to keep to himself.

Miller thought about it and decided maybe there was something he could do.

CHAPTER TWENTY-TWO

Harry Feld left CIA headquarters at Langley at his usual time and drove to his condominium in Crystal City, Virginia. He parked his Audi in the garage and unlocked the door to his home.

It was a modest place. Two bedrooms and a living room and a kitchen. He was divorced and his ex-wife lived in their old house with their two kids in Alexandria. Harry Feld paid the mortgage on the house and the condo. His son was now a student at George Mason University. One year's tuition constituted a hefty percentage of Harry's annual salary at the CIA.

Harry Feld thought he would be happier after he divorced. He was wrong. Though he had been persistently unfaithful to his wife, he found that he missed having a sort of marital home base. He had been seeing another woman steadily for the past year. Though she was a gentile and a bit of a hayseed, he sensed that he would probably marry her too. Not that he planned to be any more faithful to her than he had his first wife. But he needed the base. Needed someone to come home to. Better to hear a woman nag than to hear nothing at all. He didn't like being alone.

His home seemed empty now. He would do what he usually did. Watch ESPN for about an hour, then walk down the street to a bar and eat dinner and try to meet another woman. Any woman would do. Persistence was the key. Persistence, charm, and tenacity. Harry Feld was very optimistic when it came to women. His view was, if you were hanging from a cliff and a woman was stomping on your hands, you just told yourself she wasn't stomping as hard as she could be. And if the rejection became final, you just moved on to the next. There would always be another. Harry Feld was a big believer in high volume. And Washington was filled with lonely women.

Harry Feld popped open an organic soda and took it into the living room. He sat down and turned on the television to watch *Sports Center.* He was loosening his tie when Miller walked into the living room to join him.

Miller showed him his pistol and said, "No, remain where you are. I just want to talk to you."

"How the hell did you get in here?"

"It was easier than you know," Miller said. "A spy should be more careful about home security."

Harry Feld said, "You here to rob me? Take what you want."

"No. I'm just here to talk to you. Like I said. You will remain seated, please."

Feld leaned forward. "Who are you?"

Miller walked over to him. With his hand, Miller motioned Feld to sit back. Feld did so and Miller reached into Feld's jacket pockets. He took out Feld's cell phone. Then he took the television remote control away from Feld and took a seat across from him.

Miller muted the volume on the television.

"My name is Kurt Miller. I'm an agent with the BND."

"So you say," Feld said. "I've never heard of you."

"No, I wouldn't think so. But I know something about you that I think we should discuss."

"You come into my home with a gun so we can talk," Feld said. "Is this perhaps something we can discuss on the phone?"

"Telephones are not secure."

"And this is?"

"For me," Miller said. "You have a gun yourself, don't you? Perhaps in your bedroom? Or maybe in your refrigerator. That's where some mercenaries put them."

"I'm not a mercenary. I work for the Department of Agriculture."

"No, you work for the CIA. An analyst. Like myself, uh?"

"You tell me."

Miller smiled. Let him have some dignity, Miller thought.

Miller said, "I'll tell you what I know. Two years ago, I read an FBI report. The subsection was titled 'Foreign Economic Collection and Industrial Espionage.' In that subsection was information related to Israel's attempt to gather proprietary information on American military systems and advanced computing applications. There was evidence that Israel obtained some of this information from an American source and passed it on to China. The Chinese, in turn, used that information to develop their own J-10 aircraft fighter."

The CIA analyst stared at Miller for a few moments. "So what?"

"So we were curious about what source the Israelis used to get that information."

"I see," Feld said. "And did the FBI report give you a name?"

"Oh, of course not," Miller said. "But you already know that. Having read the report yourself."

"I don't work for the FBI, Mister . . . what is your name?"

"Miller. Kurt Miller."

"Your real name."

"That is my real name. I've got nothing to hide."

"So you read a report." Harry Feld raised his hands to suggest it wasn't much.

"Yes," Miller said. "It was not highly classified. That's why I believe you read it yourself."

"Why would a CIA analyst take the time to read an FBI report?"

"To see if they were on to him."

Feld was quiet again. He moved his mouth a bit. Then he smiled again and shook his head.

"I see," Feld said. "The Israelis got a hold of some classified information on weapons systems and naturally it was a Jew who gave it to them."

"You are Jewish?"

"Oh, don't be coy with me, Mr. Miller. You know I'm a Jew. As I know you're a German."

Miller said, "What do you mean by that?" He was angry at the suggestion.

"It only means that some things never change," Feld said. "BND, Stasi, Gestapo. You're all the same to me."

"I think you flatter yourself," Miller said. "Rabbi or priest, it makes no difference to me. Your sin is in what you did, not who you are."

Harry Feld snorted. Contemptuous, but not frightened. It made Miller feel a little better. Miller had been called Jew lover by a number of Arab suspects over the years. He'd been called a Nazi by some of the same people. They didn't seem to see the irony.

Miller said, "If I may get back to the report."

"Be my guest. But we both know that my name is nowhere to be found in that report."

"You are right," Miller said. "Your name is not in the FBI report. But it *is* in a report I wrote for my agency. You see, after we reviewed that report, we came to the conclusion that the FBI and perhaps the Americans in general were not much interested in finding out who at the CIA sold that information to the Israelis. Likely for political reasons."

"What political reasons?"

"Not wanting to damage the relationship between Israel and America. Come now, you know that already."

"Israel's interests are American interests."

Miller sighed. He'd heard that before too. And never bought it.

Miller said, "The FBI may not have been concerned about who sold the information, but we were. We like to be thorough about things like that."

"Yes, you Germans are all about being thorough."

Miller ignored that and said, "You see, we wanted to know who the spy was at the CIA. Not for the purpose of targeting anyone for arrest, but to protect ourselves. To see who the BND can trust."

"Oh, of course. Okay, I'll bite. Tell me what you found."

"I cross-referenced the FBI report with some material we had from the Mossad. In particular, some intelligence prepared by an agent named Aron Kornblidt."

Feld shifted in his seat.

Miller said, "You know him, don't you?"

"No."

"Ah, see, you are lying to me already. We know you met him in London three years ago."

"You spied on me?"

"Just as your country has spied on our Ms. Merkel. Come now, Harry. We are neither one of us virgins. Allies spy on allies. It is nothing new."

"So maybe you got a photo. Or some report from the Mossad. It doesn't prove anything."

"The report I prepared concluded that you were the one who sold the classified technology to the Israelis. The people I work for put your name in a file and put the report in a drawer. Maybe to see if they could use it at a later date."

"This is despicable. Presuming *part* of what you say is correct. Presuming *someone* at the CIA sold technology to the Israelis. You come here and point your finger at a Jew. You call me a traitor. Meaning what? A Jew can't be loyal to his country?"

Miller suppressed another sigh. "Are we back to that again?"

"You're the one making the accusation."

"This is about you, Harry. Not the Jews. Don't insult me by attempting to use that as some sort of shield."

"A shield? You—"

"And please don't speak to me of loyalty. I know you sold the information for the money, not for the homeland. We know about your spending habits. We know about the women. The expensive trips to Europe. The Range Rover you bought for one of your mistresses. The earrings you bought at Tiffany's in New York for another. It's all been documented. You're living exceptionally well on the salary of an analyst."

"I—you can't prove that."

"Prove what?"

"Where I got that money."

"Then perhaps you can," Miller said. "A deceased relative perhaps? A lottery ticket? Or maybe you won it wagering on a football game? You tell me what the plausible alternative is."

Harry Feld was quiet for a long time. He looked at the silent screen on his television, but got no help from the sports analysts. He looked back at Miller with a different expression.

"Israel is an ally," Feld said.

"Of my country as well as yours."

"Oh, don't give me that shit. You're a German."

"Living in the twenty-first century," Miller said. "Things are not as they were, Harry. Germany is Israel's largest trading partner in Europe. The largest one in the world next to the United States. And we have supplied them with almost as many weapons as America has. The Gestapo card is not going to work with me."

"Well, pardon me if I'm not sold on the new Germany. Yes, I care about the security of Israel. That doesn't make me a traitor. Nor does speaking to Aron Kornblidt."

"I know Aron," Miller said. "I rather like him, in fact. He's a tough old bastard. Passionate about his country. He makes no apologies about trying to protect Israel. He'll use whatever means he can to get information. An appeal to Israeli security, religion, and money. All three, if necessary. He is a patriot. He hasn't betrayed his country. Israel is his home. But it's not your home."

"So what? You're going to tell me I can't serve two masters? Is that it?"

"You serve who you like," Miller said. "It's not my business."

"Then what are you here for?"

"I'm here to get information."

"Or what? The BND will release your report?"

"Yes, that is about the size of it."

Feld studied the German for a while. Then he said, "You said earlier that the FBI wasn't much interested in exposing me. Presuming I am the one who did this thing. What makes you think they'll change their minds now?"

"They'll have to when it becomes public. And when that happens, you'll be facing a lifetime in prison. Like your Mr. Pollard."

"Pollard was nuts." Feld seemed to be depressed at the thought of being compared to Jonathan Pollard. Miller didn't blame him.

"Perhaps," Miller said. "But you don't have that excuse. If this sordid matter indeed goes public, you will find that Aron Kornblidt won't be there to help you. You see, he already has all he needs from you."

"What is it *you* need from me, Mr. Miller?"

"Some information about a man you used to work with,"

Miller said. "His name is Carl Tanner."

Harry Feld put his face in his hands. He did not cry, but his body sagged with defeat. After a while, he took his face out of his hands and looked back at Miller.

"I know something about Tanner," Feld said. "I can direct you to someone who knows more. Someone who had more access to the dirty secrets than I do. How much are you willing to pay?"

Miller smiled and said, "Nothing."

Chapter Twenty-Three

Gehlen heard the gunfire as soon as he got out of his car. He was in the country, somewhere between Washington and the Pennsylvania border. He'd driven down a long dirt road through a forest. He stopped his car at a gate in a fenced-off area. He called Tanner on his cell phone and Tanner sent someone down to unlock the gate.

The man who came down to open the gate was a young, burly mercenary Gehlen had never seen before. The man was stocky and wore a crewcut. He had a tattoo that covered the left side of his neck. He also had a Glock pistol in a shoulder holster.

"You Gehlen?" the man said. His tone not friendly or welcoming.

"Yeah." Gehlen was discomfited by the sight of this man, whose name was Lyle Waters. Gehlen thought Lyle looked like he had just got out of county jail. The man hadn't said much, but Gehlen seemed to detect some backwoods in the man's accent and manner. Eastern Kentucky maybe. Maybe the sort whose idea of amusement was breaking someone's arm over a tree stump. Gehlen didn't want to know much about him.

"Park your car over there," Lyle said.

Gehlen drove his BMW amidst a group of pickup trucks and muddied SUVs. Lyle closed and locked the gate behind him. Gehlen was uneasy locked in anywhere with this goon. It wasn't the same as standing on a street corner and seeing the soldiers on parade.

"Up here," Lyle said.

Gehlen followed Lyle up a trail through the woods. The trail was steeper than it looked. There were tree roots and rocks Gehlen had to step on to keep from sliding back. The mercenary in front of him wore camouflage pants and hiking boots, but Gehlen was in a suit and overcoat and a pair of black Allen Edmonds.

They trudged through the winding trail for about half a mile. They reached a plateau at the top of the hill and walked through some more trees. A couple of hundred yards of that and then the trail began to descend. They came into a rocky area with crags, creating a shelter.

"Stay to the right," Lyle said.

Tanner and four other men were under the crag, shooting at man-shaped paper targets pinned to trees about sixty yards to the left. Tanner wore headgear to protect his ears. Some of the other men didn't wear the protection. The shots echoed off the walls of rock.

One of the other men, whose name was Carter, pointed suddenly and said, "There."

Tanner raised his semi-automatic pistol in a two-handed grip and fired. About thirty yards away, a squirrel dropped from a tree. The forty-caliber bullet had taken off his head.

Grunts of approval from a couple of the men.

Tanner turned to regard Gehlen. A smile on Tanner's face. Whether it was because he was proud of his shot or because he took pleasure in Gehlen's feeling out of place, Gehlen didn't know.

"You want to fire a couple of rounds?" Tanner said.

Gehlen standing there in his mud-stained Allen Edmonds and camel-hair topcoat. Some of the hard-looking men looking at him now.

"No thanks," Gehlen said.

"Take five," Tanner said to the men.

Tanner took off his headgear and Gehlen motioned him to walk away with him. They got a few yards away from the others.

Gehlen said, "You got some real hard cases there." He felt he should say something.

"They're good men."

"Where did they come from?"

"Do you really want to know?"

"No," Gehlen said. He didn't either. Tanner might have pulled them off duty following other candidates or he might have pulled them out of Afghanistan or he might have pulled them out of a penitentiary. It was better not to know their names or where they came from.

Gehlen added, "As long as they get the job done."

Tanner turned away to hide his smile. Gehlen trying to sound tough again. Why did he have to do that?

Tanner said, "They'll get it done. It's good duty."

"So you've already told them?"

"Why wouldn't I?"

"I don't know."

"Is it because the target is a white man instead of an Arab? Let me tell you—German, Arab, or Jew—it's all the same to them. Like shooting a squirrel."

"Well, they're being paid." Gehlen again saying something just to say something.

"Thirty-thousand-dollar bonus to the one who brings down Miller," Tanner said. "Or brings him to me alive. I figure Lindsey can afford that."

"She can. But why would you want him brought to you?"

Tanner said, "I've got some things I want to ask him."

Gehlen looked back down the trail at the mercenaries. One man in a cap handing another man a flask. The man tilting his head in gratitude before he took a swig. *Christ*, Gehlen thought.

Drinking and shooting. He needed to finish his conversation with Tanner and go.

Gehlen said, "I don't understand."

"I want to know what Miller knows. Who he's spoken to. If he's left something behind to come back on us."

"You think he'd tell you?"

"Yeah."

Gehlen looked out into the woods and the pond beyond. The water stagnant.

"So you want to torture him?"

"Yeah."

Gehlen nodded. He knew Tanner was lying to him about his reasons for wanting to torture the German and Tanner knew he knew. Gehlen had defended the use of torture in print and on television appearances. He said the standard party line, that the use of torture saved American lives. He knew it didn't save lives, though, and he didn't really care. What men like Tanner and himself understood was that the primary purpose of torture was not to gain information, but to instill fear in the enemy. The enemy had to fear you. There was no other way. Tanner was a sadist who enjoyed hurting people. Gehlen, in turn, was vain enough to tell himself that he was more moral than the Tanners of this world because Gehlen himself wasn't the one doing the waterboarding. Gehlen understood the politics of torture in the way that any savvy Washington political operative did. He knew there was more tacit support of it than vocal support against it. Few, if any, politicians ever got elected by defending the Geneva Convention.

"I'm cool with that," Gehlen said. "But don't stretch it out too long. Lindsey wants this wrapped up as soon as possible."

"I understand that," Tanner said. "But we don't want any loose ends. Those guys down there, they may just be nameless assassins. Hired guns you're not going to remember. But Miller knows my name."

"Well . . ."

"He knows your name too."

"Yeah, you've told me that already."

Tanner raised a hand. "I'm on your side, Jay. Neither of us wants to be compromised."

Gehlen shook his head. "I don't even know that he's still here."

"You think he left the country?"

"I would in his place."

"You're not him," Tanner said. "Why do you think he's still here?"

"You told me Lindsey said he wants two million now. Who would leave when there's that much money in the till?"

Gehlen said, "That's a fair point. He could have killed Lindsey in Virginia. He didn't."

"Because he wants the money. Lindsey's no good to him dead."

"I know, but . . . something's off. You still got that phone he gave you?"

"Yeah."

"Why hasn't he called you then? Why hasn't he called you and told you to meet him someplace so you can pay him that money?"

"Because he knows if I see him again, I'll kill him. He's going to try to find some other way to get the money."

Gehlen said, "Not long ago, you suggested we pay him and be done with him."

"I said that was an option. But since then, he's doubled the price. Two million, one million, it makes no difference to me. It's not my money. But upping the stakes shows he's not being reasonable. So maybe it's time we quit being reasonable."

Gehlen took another look at the mercenaries and thought

they had more to do with Tanner changing his mind than Miller's greed. Tanner had strength in numbers now. Tanner shooting heads off squirrels and talking about torturing the German. If the German wasn't anything to worry about, why had Tanner gathered all these men? What did they really know about Miller?

Gehlen said, "Does it bother you that Miller got so close to Lindsey?"

"Doesn't it bother you?"

"It bothered her."

"We got a foreign national on American soil threatening the next leader of our country," Tanner said. "Whether you know it or not, Horvath's not going to settle for anything less than his corpse. You let Miller live, she'll hold it against you. She'll hold it against me too."

For the first time, Gehlen wondered if Lindsey had spoken with Tanner alone. Gehlen had always comforted himself with the notion that he was a mediator between Tanner and Lindsey Horvath. The highly valued middleman. But . . . what if he wasn't always in the middle?

For quite some time now, Lindsey had made no secret of the fact that she wanted her own secret police. Once she was President, she would never appoint someone like Tanner to head the CIA or the FBI. Tanner had too many skeletons for that. Tanner was not the sort of man you could put before a Senate subcommittee. But she would want Tanner working for her in secret. He would remain a highly useful resource to her. With that in mind, who knew what she and Tanner had said to each other? What promises had been made?

It would not be above Tanner to suggest to Gehlen that they pay Miller and then, after Gehlen, agreed to it, Tanner would tell Lindsey that it had been *Gehlen's* idea to pay Miller. That would make Gehlen look weak to Lindsey. It might even make Lindsey think Tanner was more valuable to her than he was.

With Lindsey, you always had to prove your utility as much as your loyalty.

But maybe he was overthinking it. Tanner was muscle. A bag-man and a killer who could summon cold-eyed goons on a few hours' notice. He didn't have Gehlen's political skills. Lindsey would always need someone to navigate Washington.

Still . . . it wouldn't be out of character for Lindsey to play him and Tanner against each other. If anything, just to keep them both in check. Gehlen was quietly embarrassed that he hadn't thought of that before.

Tanner looking at him now.

"What's the matter?" Tanner said.

"Nothing," Gehlen said. "I'm just wondering if Miller's still here."

"He's here," Tanner said.

CHAPTER TWENTY-FOUR

The German Shepherd remained on the ground of the driveway with his paws in front of him, but his ears cocked erect as Miller came into view. The German shepherd watching the German as the German came to a stop. He was a handsome animal, with the long fur you saw more in the European breeds. The dog didn't growl or show aggression, but Miller still regarded him carefully and thought, *that one is ready.*

A man of about sixty came out from behind an old Chevy with two-toned paint. The old man looked at Miller then snapped his fingers at the dog and said "Okay, Bear."

The German shepherd lowered his head and relaxed.

The man said, "Something I can do for you, friend?"

"My name is Miller. I used to work for the German government. Are you Colonel Toomey?"

"I am."

"I was wondering if I could have a word with you."

Colonel Toomey wiped his fingers on a yellow cloth. He was a big man with big hands. A John Wayne figure, but balding.

The Colonel said, "What about?"

"Carl Tanner."

Colonel Toomey stared at him for a while. He didn't seem like he was in a hurry. Toomey said, "Is he a friend of yours?"

"No."

"Well, that's good to hear. Are you a reporter?"

"No. I was an intelligence analyst for the BND."

"Was?"

"I was terminated. Tanner and some of his friends were responsible."

"Is that so?" Toomey said. "You think I had something to do with that?"

"I doubt it."

"What do you want with me then?"

"A man I'll not call a friend told me you might have some information on him."

"What man is that?"

"His name is Harry Feld."

The old man laughed. "God Almighty, you trust *him*?"

"Hardly. But one takes what one can get."

Colonel Toomey grunted.

"Pretty dog," Miller said.

"Bear's handsome, but he isn't much of a watchdog. Burglar comes snooping around, he hides under the bed. Which means I have to protect myself with a shotgun."

A veiled threat there. Miller understood it. He was glad he'd left the Ruger in the glove compartment of his car.

"Well, as long as the dog isn't hurt," Miller said.

Colonel Toomey smiled and shook his head. "You're a soldier, aren't you?"

"I was. How did you know that?"

"We know each other. You've got some story to tell me, I guess."

"Perhaps."

"Well, let's go into the house and have a beer. If you can stomach American beer."

The dog lay on the kitchen floor while the soldiers sat at the table. Miller told Colonel Toomey most of what happened. Miller sipped from a can of Natural Light while the old colonel sucked down two cans between bites of salt-and-vinegar chips.

Toomey said, "Before you worked in intelligence, that's when you were a soldier, right?"

"That's right."

"GSG-9?"

Miller said, "Why would you say that?"

"I think I've heard about you. From the Israelis. They say you were good. Very good."

"It was a long time ago."

"Are you kin to Ernst Miller?"

The German stared at the American for a moment.

"Don't look uncomfortable," Toomey said. "It wasn't your war."

"He was my grandfather."

The old soldier smiled. "Man. Ernst Miller's grandson at my house. This is turning out to be a good day."

"For you, perhaps. My grandfather was a Nazi."

"Nazi, maybe. But a hell of a soldier. Do you know I wrote an essay about him when I was at West Point? We studied the Battle of Villers-Bocage. He took out fourteen tanks and fifteen personnel carriers in about half an hour."

"It was fifteen minutes, actually."

"Really?"

"That's the myth, anyway. In certain parts of Germany, it may be ten minutes."

Toomey laughed.

"Well, you're a good old boy. Ten minutes. Hey, have you read *Panzer Commander*?"

"Yes."

"I've read that book so many times, I can't count. I met von Luck in Hamburg. He signed a copy for me. Did you ever meet him?"

"No."

"That's too bad. God, he must have been at least seventy when I met him. We were at a restaurant and there was a waitress who was serving him couldn't have been more than twenty-five. She had no idea who he was or what he'd done and she was *flirting* with him. He was embarrassed by it. But he owned that table. Handsome fellah. Very aristocratic, very smooth. You remind me of him."

Miller made a gesture. He didn't know whether to be flattered or ashamed. Well . . . probably he was flattered. Hans von Luck, the officer Rommel admired and treated like a son. Most contemporary officers in the German army had heard stories of his compassion and devotion to his men. Von Luck fought the North African campaign and would order a ceasefire at five o'clock every day so that the German and the British forces could both rest. Any British soldier captured by von Luck's outfit could be assured of humane treatment. Von Luck was known for contacting the British on his radio and letting them know that they had "found" one of their men and that he was safe and secure. Von Luck's regiment once ran out of cigarettes and he'd learned through intelligence that the British Army had just received a shipment of cigarettes. Von Luck radioed the British and offered to release one of their captive officers in exchange for a million cigarettes. The British countered with an offer of 600,000 cigarettes and von Luck agreed. But then the British officer *refused* to be released because he felt he was worth at least a million. Funny people, the English. Clinging to their snobbish pride even during a war. Like Toomey, Miller liked to think that von Luck was a good man fighting for an unworthy cause. But then there was always the possibility that von Luck was a born charmer. Certainly he had style. Colonel Toomey was not the first American to be taken with him.

Miller said, "Feld said you were a tank man yourself."

"Oh, yeah. Took out a few tanks of the Iraqi Revolutionary Guard."

"I heard it was more than a few. About sixty. And you had only fifteen tanks to do it."

"Well, they were only Iraqis. They're cruel sons of bitches, but bone-ass worthless as soldiers."

Miller said, "I don't know that modesty becomes you."

"I'm hardly modest. For me, the important thing is that we had no American casualties."

"Yes, that's the important thing."

"God help the man who loves soldiering." Toomey raised his beer can. "To the dogs of war."

"Cry havoc," Miller said and raised his own can.

"Now how the hell did you ever get mixed up with a shitbird like Tanner?"

"Like I told you, he came into my world."

"Well, I don't doubt he had you put in jail. He's capable of that and worse. But you're not going to get anyone to believe it."

"You believe it."

"Well, I'm a very intelligent man for a dumbass from Arkansas. And I know Tanner."

Miller said, "What is it you know?"

"Like I told you, my specialty is tanks. But for a time they had me in Special Forces. The CIA would call us in to hot spots from time to time. We'd take a camp, then a CIA counter-terrorist team would come in and do the dirty shit."

"Like what?"

Toomey eyed the German across the table. "You know what."

"Torture captives?"

"Oh, we don't call it torture here. It's enhanced interrogation."

"Ah."

"You disapprove?"

"Don't you?"

Toomey shrugged. "I've never taken part in it myself. But I suppose I'm as guilty as anyone because I knew it was going on and didn't report it. There were times I could have pulled back the curtain to see what was going on, and I chose to leave the curtain alone. I let my ambition and military career get the better of me. You see, most Americans don't want to hear that we torture. That's something the Germans did. That's something terrorists do. Americans don't do it."

"You just said—"

"I know what I said. You're not hearing me. Why do you think Tanner did things like that? You think he's dumb enough to do it without first protecting himself? Kurt, they had memorandums from White House lawyers telling them their 'enhanced interrogation' techniques were legal. They had authorization. They were cleared *before* the fact. Not a war crime if the Justice Department says it's legal. Now it's passed and they say they've stopped the torture. And maybe they have. But no way you're going to file criminal charges on Carl Tanner or anyone else at the CIA. Because if you do, the first thing he'll say is he was authorized to do it from the Justice Department. The Justice Department isn't going to put itself on trial."

"And you?"

"I'm a guy who joined the Army because I fell in love with tanks. I'm bloodthirsty and savage and I wanted to be a tank officer. So I kept my head down and my mouth shut until I could get command of a tank regiment. I'm really no better than any of them."

"I don't know about that."

"I do. Son, you know your country's history. Are the Germans really a savage people?"

"They certainly were."

"In war time. I read history too. Even Hitler knew he couldn't get away with killing all those Jews until he had the cover of war. When I was younger, I believed in something called fighting clean. Some of your German officers believed in that too. Von Luck, Rommel. But fighting clean in a war is an illusion. You become dehumanized and you end up doing things you never thought you were capable of. You lose yourself. You don't like the atrocity that comes with wars, you don't start wars."

"Is Tanner still in the CIA?"

"No. He was bounced out."

Miller said, "How does one get bounced out of the CIA?"

"I'm not exactly sure. Rumor is, he was caught stealing money he was supposed to deliver to an Afghan chief. The chief was killed and the money disappeared. They couldn't prove it was him, but they suggested he retire anyway. You see, they can tolerate a sadist, but not a thief."

"What's he doing now?"

"He runs his own private security firm. More dangerous now than he ever was. Certainly, he's richer."

"You are retired now?"

"It was suggested to me that I retire. In the modern Army, you're not allowed to speak honestly about what wars are ill-advised. Not if you want to get promoted."

"Is the war in Syria ill-advised?"

"Oh, hell yeah."

"And if you'd gone along with it . . ."

"I'd still be in uniform."

Miller said, "And the tank victory in Iraq?"

"Yesterday's papers. Oh, they gave me a medal for it. And I'm embarrassed to say that I was proud to get it. But they always give out medals when a war becomes unpopular. It was certainly no guarantee of a favorable career."

Miller thought of his grandfather's Iron Cross. The disappointment he'd felt when his father had told him he had disposed of it. Ernst Miller, the dead hero of the Third Reich.

Miller said, "I think Tanner killed Paul Posner."

"That's what you've told me. And I believe that too. Knowing Tanner, he killed Posner because he thought Posner had something on him. Something that may not have even had anything to do with you."

"I've considered that."

"But it doesn't really matter, Kurt. You're not going to be able to prove Tanner killed him. You're certainly not going to be able to tie it to Jay Gehlen or Lindsey Horvath. You want Tanner off your back, you're going to have to kill him. I'm sorry to tell you that, but that's how it is. You got a weapon?"

"Yes. A Ruger revolver. It's in the car."

Colonel Toomey smiled again. "Good gun. But I'm glad you didn't bring it into my home. Bear wouldn't have liked that."

And now Miller smiled. Mauled by a killer dog or cut down by Colonel Toomey's shotgun. And neither one would have hesitated.

"I wouldn't have liked that either," Miller said.

Chapter Twenty-Five

Harry Feld looked at the photo and said, "Yeah, that's the guy. He's a little older now. Thinner." Harry Feld smiled. "Maybe American food doesn't agree with him."

Tanner didn't smile and said, "He hasn't been here that long. He was in a British prison for a year. Did he tell you that?"

Feld tried to mask his surprise. He didn't want Tanner to think he had missed something. "No, he didn't. He led me to believe he was still working for German intelligence."

"He's not," Tanner said. "Not by a damn sight."

They were at a restaurant in Crystal City. They sat at a booth while Harry ate nachos from a large plate. Harry using one chip to scrape the excess sour cream off the top. Tanner had come to meet him after Harry called him. Tanner's man Lyle sat at the bar sipping from a bottle of Budweiser.

Harry Feld said, "Yeah, I kind of figured that."

"You did?" Tanner said. He didn't believe him. Tanner said, "How did you know if he didn't tell you?"

"I've been working in intelligence for a long time. I knew there wasn't something right about him. That's why I called you."

"He broke into your home?"

"Yeah."

"How did he do that?"

"I don't know, actually. I've got an alarm system."

"Why did you talk to him then?"

"Well, he was armed. Not that that bothered me." Harry Feld shrugged. Letting Tanner know he was a veteran who had seen it all. Or something.

"Didn't, huh?"

"Oh, fuck no," Feld said. "I knew this kraut was up to something. He talked to me like he had something on me. Something to blackmail me with. It was bullshit, of course. He hadn't done his homework. But I didn't let him know that. So I worked him and let him think I was worried and used that to find out what he was up to."

"And what is that?"

"Excuse me?"

"What is it he's up to? In your opinion."

"Well, he wanted to know about you."

"What is it he wanted to know?"

"Who you were. Where you work. Whether or not you're still in the CIA."

"And what did you tell him?"

Harry Feld put on his serious expression. "Hey, I didn't tell him shit. Besides, I don't know what it is you've been doing since you left the Agency. I mean, even if I'd wanted to tell him things—and I didn't—I didn't have anything to tell."

"I see."

"Well, I hope you see. We're on the same side, you and I. Anyway, I'm glad I called you. I knew there was something wrong with that guy."

A chubby waitress in her early twenties came to the table to refill their drinks. Tanner shook his head when she asked him if he wanted more coffee. Harry Feld said to the girl, "You staying out of trouble?"

The waitress gave him a forced smile and said, "Yeah, I guess." She had no interest in bantering with this man who was older than her father.

194

Her discomfort had no effect on Feld. Little could deter him when he wanted to engage.

"You're new here, aren't you?"

"Yeah. I started last week."

"You go to school?"

Before she could answer, Tanner said, "That'll be all, thank you."

Tanner's voice was firm and a little bit threatening. The waitress left. Feld frowned and Tanner said, "Pipe it later, huh? We're in the middle of something."

"Sorry, Carl."

"Did you tell anyone at work about Miller's visit to you?"

"No. I just called you."

"Why not?"

"Why not what?"

"Why didn't you tell anyone at the Agency?"

Feld held one of the nachos between his mouth and the dish. "I didn't see the point."

"Protocol says you're supposed to report that sort of thing. After all, Miller is a foreign agent."

"I thought you said he wasn't with BND anymore?"

"I don't think he is, but you never know."

"I don't understand. Are you saying I should report it?"

Jesus Christ, Tanner thought. Why did the Agency let people like this in? The man had to be spoon-fed every little thing.

"No," Tanner said, "you shouldn't report it. Ever. Do you understand me?"

"Yeah, I understand."

Tanner saw it a little more clearly now. He said, "So what was it he had on you?"

"Excuse me?"

"You said he tried to blackmail you. With what?"

"Oh. It was something about a woman I'm involved with. It

didn't mean shit to me and I told him so."

"Okay," Tanner said. Though he didn't believe that either. The German had something on Feld. And it probably had nothing to do with pussy. Still, Tanner felt better. Now he had confirmation the German was still in the States. That was good.

Tanner said, "Did he tell you where he was staying?"

"No," Feld said. "But I'll tell you something. He fucked up. He parked his car in the condo lot. The lot has a camera security system. I have access to that, so I know what he's driving."

"You got the make of the car?"

"Yeah. And the tag. He's driving a green Jaguar XJ6. Pennsylvania plates."

Feld slid a piece of paper across the booth. The auto information written on it. Tanner resisted the urge to grin. The fat man trying to play spy now. Why not wrap the note in a newspaper? Make it more clandestine.

Tanner put the note in his jacket pocket.

Feld said, "Listen, Carl. I understand you've got your own security company now. I was wondering if, you know, you need people."

"You got your twenty in?"

"I will in two months," Feld said. "All these Agency guys are flocking to the independent contractors, getting twice the pay. Christ, you see some of them in the Agency cafeteria. Wearing their contractor badges and getting paid double to do the same work. It makes you sick."

Tanner said, "We can always use an experienced man. Can I call you next week?"

"Sure."

Tanner shook his hand and thanked him for his help.

At the bar, Tanner tapped Lyle on the arm and said something to him. Harry Feld did not notice Lyle looking back at him before he finished his beer and left.

★ ★ ★ ★ ★

Feld got the waitress to open up to him a little bit. She told him she was from Ellicott City, Maryland. She told him she was studying cosmetology and that her sister ran a men's hair salon in Alexandria near the mall. Her sister didn't take women customers and only took cash payments. The waitress was guileless and never intuited that Feld was working her. Harry Feld took this in and decided he would not ask her for her number this time. He would see her again. Sometimes it paid to be patient. The key was to get them to feel comfortable.

It was raining when he left. Cars whisked by on the wet street as Harry Feld walked to his Audi. It was late now, dark and cold, and he was alone on the sidewalk. He wished he hadn't left his umbrella in his car. He would dry off when he got home and then he would call his girlfriend.

The Audi was parked on the side of the street at the end of a line of cars. After he passed a Chevy Suburban, a dark figure came up from the seat.

Harry Feld walked behind his Audi and into the street. He pressed his key fob to unlock the car and heard the beep.

"Harry," a voice said.

Harry Feld turned around to see Lyle Waters about fifteen feet behind him. Lyle closed the distance and raised the pistol with a long silencer and shot Harry Feld in the chest. Feld dropped and Lyle stepped next to him and shot him three more times in the face and neck.

CHAPTER TWENTY-SIX

Mrs. Posner said, "I guess I should start by saying something that may surprise you."

"What's that?" Miller said.

"That when I last saw you, I was furious about what you said to me. The stuff about the self-loathing and the drinking. I wanted to kill you for that."

Miller said, "Please forget that I said those things."

"No, they needed to be said. My name is Anne, by the way. You don't have to call me Mrs. Posner anymore."

They were at a coffee shop in Chevy Chase. It was relatively bohemian for the neighborhood. It had dark corners and old scratched wood tables and furniture that didn't match. Skinny college students with long hair worked the sales counter. Miller liked the place.

Miller said, "It surprised me that you would agree to meet with me a second time."

Miller had called her from his cell phone that morning. He had left a message on her land line. He didn't have her cell number. He didn't expect to get a return call, but was glad when he did.

"I didn't really agree to meet with you the first time," Anne Posner said. "You just showed up on my doorstep. Anyway, the surprising thing I wanted to say to you is that I'm grateful to you for what you said to me."

Miller looked at her. Anne Posner looked better today. There were no guilty circles under her eyes. Her skin was clear. Her hair was pulled back in a ponytail. She looked like she hadn't had a drink in a week.

Miller said, "That is a surprise."

"Maybe I should elaborate a little. Are you married, Mr. Miller?"

"No. I was."

"Any children?"

"No."

"Was your wife—was she faithful to you?"

"Yes, I believe. I was unfaithful to her, though. We were separated at the time, but that is no real excuse. I was not a very good husband to her."

"I was unfaithful to my partner as well. But you already knew that."

"It's none of my business."

"I know it's not, but for some reason I want to tell you something about it. Do you mind?"

"No."

"Did you ever want something and then get it and then find out you didn't really want it?"

"I suppose."

Anne Posner smiled. "Well, that's not much of an answer. But anyway, I thought I wanted to be a wife and a mother. I was sure Paul and I wanted the same things. But I think we were mismatched from the beginning. Or maybe I wasn't really good enough for him. Anyway, he was gone a lot, we weren't really talking to each other much, and I got depressed. Very depressed. I went to a counselor and she just wanted to prescribe me a lot of drugs. I said no, I thought that would just make the problem worse. Or avoid diagnosing what the real problem was. Or repress the feelings I had that maybe I needed to feel. I mean, you can't feel the good if you don't feel the bad, right?"

"Yes."

"So the counselor, instead of suggesting an alternative, just got angry at me for not taking her advice. For not taking the pills. And Paul . . . Paul got mad at me too. He said, 'Just take the damn pills.' So then I felt that the two of them were ganging up on me. I felt bullied. And I felt alone. And then I met a man who I thought was kind and interesting and I had an affair with him."

"The man who called you the other day?"

"Yes. I'm—I'm taking a break from him now. I quit drinking and I started to see things a little more clearly. My boyfriend—I guess I should say my ex-boyfriend now—he didn't like that. You see, he drinks too. You quit drinking and you lose your drinking friends. You know?"

"I know," Miller said, though he had never been a heavy drinker. You didn't have to be a recovering alcoholic to recognize common sense.

"So I'm out of what I think was a not very healthy relationship. And now that I'm not drinking or looking forward to the next drink, I'm a little scared and a little lonely."

"Sometimes a little loneliness is not such a bad thing."

"I've always been lonely, just too sedated to realize it. I refused to take anti-depressants and instead took to the wine and sedated myself that way. And I probably got my husband killed."

Miller shook his head. "You didn't do that."

"But if he hadn't gone to the liquor store—"

"If he hadn't gone to the liquor store, they would have got him someplace else. At a convenience store or in the parking lot of a coffee shop. So please stop this talk of getting your husband killed."

Anne Posner sighed and stared into her coffee cup. She said, "You still think he was assassinated, don't you?"

"I know he was."

"But the police—"

"The police don't know what I know. It's been confirmed since I last saw you. A former CIA agent named Carl Tanner killed him. It was not, as you say, some gangbanger who did that. It was a gangster. A gangster working for the government. And that's the worst kind there is."

"I don't want this," Anne said. "I don't want to know this."

"Why not?"

"Because it's too goddamned scary. It's too much to comprehend. I don't want to think that governments kill their own citizens. That doesn't happen here."

"It can happen anywhere. Although until a while ago, I thought America would be the last place it would happen. No, Mrs. Posner, I don't think the United States knocked down the Twin Towers in New York. No reasonable person believes that. I'm as skeptical as the next man about government conspiracies. But there are people here with a very unpleasant agenda and they won't hesitate to stop those who are in their way."

"What people?"

"If I told you, you wouldn't believe me. I have trouble believing it myself."

"What people?"

"Tanner is working for your candidate Lindsey Horvath. In fact, I believe she gave the order to have your husband killed."

"But that's . . . that's insane."

"It is. *She's* insane, Mrs. Posner. I don't mean just right wing. Right wing, left wing, the distinction is meaningless to me. Power is power and terror is terror. People speak of Lenin as left and Hitler as right, but there was little difference between them. Terror and murder were their chosen tools."

"If this is true . . . if this is true, what are you going to do about it?"

"What do you want me do about it?"

Anne Posner frowned. "What the hell do you mean by that?"

"You have stopped drinking," Miller said. "You have ended your relationship with another alcoholic. Okay, then, I commend you for that. But now you want to carry on and forget about all this unpleasantness?"

"I didn't say that."

"Are you sure?"

"Goddamn you. I agreed to meet with you, didn't I? Why do you think I did that?"

"I'm not sure."

"Okay, I was a shitty wife. Guilty as charged."

"I didn't say—"

"Let me finish, okay? I let Paul down. No, not because I got him killed, but because I betrayed him while he was still around. You come into my life and tell me it wasn't some random act, but something planned and deliberate. And maybe you're the one who's insane. But I'm here, aren't I? I'm willing to hear what you have to say."

"All right, then."

"Just don't judge me. Not anymore."

"I won't. I'm sorry."

Anne Posner sighed again. "God, this is some mess we're in, huh?"

"It is that."

Anne said, "You think what happened to you had something to do with what happened to my husband."

"I did think that," Miller said. "Now I'm not so sure."

Anne frowned. "What do you mean?"

"I think we were targeted by the same people, yes, but now I'm beginning to wonder if your husband knew about something else. Something else Tanner and Horvath were into."

"And you want to know if I know what that was."

"I was hoping."

The widow shook her head. "I told you before, he didn't talk to me."

"About his work?"

"About much of anything."

Miller had to look at the woman again. About forty years old and very attractive without the wine and the self-pity. He had written her off as lost and weak the first time he encountered her. Now he thought he may have misread her. Maybe she had just lost sight of herself, lost sight of who she was. He was certainly not in a place to judge her for infidelity. Maybe neither one of them was suited for marriage.

Miller said, "Your husband . . . did he leave you anything?"

Anne Posner smiled. "Are you worried?"

"I'm just asking."

"He left me everything he had. It wasn't much. But I'm comfortable, if that's what you mean. I was comfortable before I met him. Family money."

"Oh."

"If you were thinking of rescuing me from poverty, I'm sorry to disappoint you."

"I . . ."

"Oh, don't be wounded. It doesn't become you. Anyway, something tells me you're not exactly the sort of man who's looking for a woman to take care of."

Miller didn't respond to that one. He said, "Do you work?"

"I was working for a lobbyist when I met him. I have a law degree, but I never practiced law. I was in something called management consulting."

"Oh."

"Yeah, it was as dull as it sounds. They'd take me back if I wanted to go, but working in Washington doesn't really appeal to me anymore. Do you know much about D.C.?"

"A little. I worked security for the German embassy a few years ago."

"How was that?"

"Dull."

Anne said, "Washington's a very insular town. There's definitely a Beltway mentality. A prevailing sense of superiority. Just about everyone who works inside it never thinks about anything outside of it. All the politicians claim to hate it, but they're no more interested in returning to Kansas or Ohio than they would be in working at a factory. They love power and this is a city of power and influence. There are exceptions, of course. There's a senator who used to be here who was very powerful and he was a good man. He was a Democrat from a southern state back when they voted for Democrats. Anyway, he saw the tea leaves and moved back home to run a university. He's happier now than he's ever been. But men like that are the exception."

"And what about you?"

"What about me?"

"You don't want power?"

The woman laughed. "Are you serious? Look at me. I'm a misfit. Believe me, I have plenty of flaws, but lust for power isn't one of them."

"I don't think you're a misfit."

Anne looked at her coffee cup again. "Well, that's kind of you, but . . ."

Miller realized he had made her uncomfortable. Perhaps she thought he was coming on to her. Perhaps he was coming on to her.

Miller said, "Are you from here?"

"No. I'm from Pittsburgh. I came here about twenty years

ago to go to college. George Washington. I'm probably going to move back to Pittsburgh. I have a sister there and she's got great kids. In a way, you might take some credit for this."

"Pardon?"

"Well, like I said before, when you quit drinking, you have to quit hanging around with people who still drink. Tony—that's my ex-boyfriend—is probably an alcoholic too. If I didn't see that before, I see it now. So there's really nothing to keep me here anymore. When I was in college, I looked down on Pittsburgh. I thought it was too unsophisticated. A dirty steel town. But it hasn't really been dirty for a long time. And I was immature when I thought such things. You know how the young can be."

"Sometimes."

"Have you been to Pittsburgh?"

"No."

"It's got all these lovely bridges. And I can get a great house there for about a tenth of what it would cost here. And it's so much safer. In D.C. you can't ride a bicycle without getting mugged."

"I think it sounds like a good idea, moving back," Miller said. "But I don't see what it has to do with me."

"You don't, do you? Well, deploying your saber-like Teutonic tact, you basically told me to quit drinking and feeling sorry for myself."

"That was thoughtless of me. Please forget that I said those things."

"I'm not exactly thanking you," Anne said. "Not directly. Yes, you were rude. But I needed to hear it from someone."

Miller shrugged again. He was thinking of his ex-wife and of Hamburg. Another city on water. He found himself envying Anne Posner for her newfound sense of home and purpose.

Miller said, "I wish you luck, madam."

"Madam? Please call me Anne, will you?"

"Anne."

"That's better. Listen, I returned your call because I have something that may help you. I—I think Paul was seeing another woman. I didn't tell you that before because I didn't think it was any of your business. I'm still not sure it is. But maybe it had something to do with him being murdered."

"Why would you think that?"

"I don't know. As you know, I kept secrets from him, so I wasn't all too keen on asking him what secrets he was keeping from me. But he was preoccupied by something. And maybe it had to do with this person he was seeing." Anne Posner looked at Miller and said, "I mean, it may be something you'd want to look into."

"And you would help me do this?"

Anne said, "I owe him something."

CHAPTER TWENTY-SEVEN

Tanner's man from the National Security Agency called him while he was eating lunch with Lyle Waters at an Olive Garden in Alexandria. Tanner had asked the guy at NSA to track the cellular phone Miller had used to call him at Bryant Park.

The guy from NSA said, "You think your man's still using the same phone?"

Tanner said, "Yeah. We've got confirmation he's still in the country."

"Well, whoever has it used it this morning to make a call to a number in Chevy Chase. The number he called is Anne Posner. I've pinged him and I think he's still in the area."

"Chevy Chase?"

"Yeah."

"Is he at Posner's house?"

"Well, the technology won't give me that much. But he's in Chevy Chase."

"Thanks."

Tanner clicked off the phone. Lyle was mopping up cream fettuccine sauce with a roll.

Tanner said, "Call Carter and have him bring the crew to Chevy Chase."

Chapter Twenty-Eight

Anne said, "I don't feel comfortable doing this."

Miller said, "Why not?"

"It's private. He didn't look at my e-mails. He didn't check the text messages on my phone."

"How do you know he didn't?"

They were sitting at the kitchen table in Anne Posner's home. Miller was looking at Paul Posner's e-mail on his personal computer. It had taken Miller only a few minutes to bust through the password. Miller had experience in such things. Miller was looking at the computer screen, not at the widow Posner.

Anne said, "That's a nasty thing to say."

"Sorry."

"No, you're not."

"Okay, I am sorry for suggesting your husband did not respect your privacy. I had no basis for saying that. But I need to know who he was in touch with."

"I didn't know you would ask for something like this when I offered to help you."

Miller almost said, "And now you do." But he didn't. He had changed his mind about Anne Posner. She was a woman of character and she hadn't asked to be mixed up in this. But certain things had to be done.

Miller said, "If it is painful for you . . ."

"Oh, just get on with what you have to do."

Miller watched her as she left the table and went to the refrigerator. He was glad to see her take out a bottle of water instead of a bottle of wine.

A few minutes later, Miller said, "There are some messages from a woman named Gina. Do you know who that is?"

"No."

Miller played with the keyboard some more. "Gina Canale. Does that sound familiar?"

"No."

"I think I have a number here," Miller said.

He called the number. Anne Posner tipped her water bottle into her mouth while she looked at the computer screen.

A young woman answered the phone. "Miss Berry's Flower Shop."

"I'm looking for Gina," Miller said.

"We don't take personal calls," the girl said.

Miller said, "But it's most important that I speak to her."

"You're no more important than anyone else," the girl said.

After a moment, Miller said, "Is this something we shouldn't discuss over the phone?"

"Go through the regular channels," the girl said.

"I understand, Miss. Shall I give you my number?"

"That would be fine."

Gina Canale returned his call about eight minutes later. She said she couldn't discuss details on the phone, but the cost for her time was fifteen hundred minimum and what they did with that time was their business and no one else's. She told him they could meet at the Marriott Hotel downtown and that of course he would be responsible for the cost of the room.

Miller said that would be fine.

He clicked off the phone and Anne said, "She agreed to meet with you?"

"Yes."

"Why would she do that?"

Miller looked at her and said, "I think she needs the money."

After a moment, Anne Posner said, "Oh, God."

Miller asked her to come with him. Anne said, "Why? You want me to watch?"

"Don't be childish."

"I'm not being childish. I'm angry. Can you understand that?"

"It's important that we talk with this woman. I can understand you being angry, but he would not have been the first to go to a prostitute."

"He was my husband."

"If it makes you uncomfortable, you can wait in the lobby. But I think you should know what she has to say. For all we know, she may have been used to compromise him."

"Compromise him. Shit."

"Will you come with me?"

"Yeah, I'll come."

Miller backed the Jaguar out of her driveway. Anne put on her seatbelt when they backed into the street. Miller drove south on the street for two blocks and then made a left turn onto another street into heavy traffic.

About a minute later, a Chevy Suburban and a black Mercedes came down from the north and stopped in front of Anne Posner's house. Tanner and his men got out of the vehicles and began to approach the house.

CHAPTER TWENTY-NINE

Gina Canale said, "Look, if you want to sit here and just talk to me, you still have to pay. But whatever it is you want to do, you better hurry up. You are only getting two hours or until you shoot off. That's the deal."

Miller sat at the table in the hotel room. Gina Canale stood at the window looking out at the Washington Monument. She was about thirty-five and she had had her breasts lifted. She wore a stylish black overcoat and slacks and an untucked white shirt under a black cashmere sweater. She was stylish, Miller thought. Though many Italian whores were stylish.

Miller said, "I understand. I like to talk first. It makes me comfortable."

"You are German?"

"Yes."

After a moment, she shrugged and said, "Well, I guess that's okay."

She took off her coat and lay on the bed. Miller stayed at his seat at the table. She looked up at the ceiling for a while. Then she said, "What do you want to tell me?"

"Not much to tell."

"What do you want me tell you?"

Miller smiled. "Anything you like."

The Italian woman said, "I was in Berlin once. When I was nineteen. I was modeling then. I posed naked in front of this art class. The students painted me. Some of them had talent. I did that for nothing."

"Hmmm."

"I posed for this book published in Germany. It was called *Love and Joy.* Or *Love and Freude.* Whatever you people say. It was an educational book. A lover's guide."

"I'm sure it was."

"You ever been to Spain?"

"Yes."

She put her hand down her pants. "I went to Barcelona with a friend and we met this old man who paid us to eat our pussies. That old man had some energy."

Miller sighed. What the girl was doing depressed him more than excited him. "Okay, that's enough."

Her expression changed to anger, the performance over. "Man, what is your fuckin' problem? What did you come here for?"

She was not scared of him, Miller saw. And that was good. He didn't want her calling the police.

Miller said, "I came here to talk to you about Paul Posner."

The Italian woman sat up in bed. She was still unafraid. Miller wondered how long it had been since she had felt fear. Since she had felt anything.

"I don't talk about clients," she said.

"This one was murdered."

"I don't know anything about that. Are you a cop or something?"

"I'm a federal agent with the German government."

"A German agent?"

"Yes."

"Then what you doing here?"

"Investigating a murder."

"In America?"

"Yes."

"I think you're lying."

"I don't much care what you think, Madam. Mr. Posner was in touch with you and perhaps it may have had something to do with him getting killed."

"What fucking business is it of yours?"

"You tell me what you know and it might keep you out of trouble."

"Maybe it keep you out of trouble too, uh?"

"I'm not the one in trouble," Miller said. He let it lay there, seeing how she would react.

Gina Canale turned and put her feet on the floor. She looked at the German for a while. Then she said, "He wasn't a client. He wanted something more from me."

Miller thought of Posner's wife. He had left her at the hotel bar. He had stayed with her until she ordered a cup of coffee. She had seen his relief when she didn't order a drink and it annoyed her. She said, "Just go, will you? I don't need you monitoring me." Now Miller wondered if she would feel any better knowing that her husband had been faithful to her after all.

Miller said to the prostitute, "What do you mean, more?"

"He wanted to know something about a friend of mine."

"What friend?"

"An old friend of mine. A good man. Your friend Posner, he wasn't very smart. He thought I might be willing to blackmail this friend." Gina Canale smiled. "He thought it would be easy. But this old friend of mine, he knows all the tricks."

"This friend of yours, is he a man of some influence?"

"Fuck yes. You say you some kind of a secret agent?"

"Not so secret."

"Then maybe you heard of him. His name is Nizar Khaled." The Italian woman smiled. It was not a pleasant sight.

Miller took it in. He said, "The arms dealer?"

213

"Yeah." She seemed very pleased with herself, knowing this man.

And maybe she had a right to be pleased. Nizar Khaled was only one of the richest men in the world. A Saudi of Kurdish and Syrian descent. Khaled had gotten an MBA from Yale and gone on to build shopping centers in the States and Europe. He then made a much bigger fortune brokering deals between the United States and Saudi Arabia. His clients included some of the largest defense contractors in America. German intelligence had reams of files on him, as did all the intelligence agencies in Europe and the States. It was well known that Khaled had developed contacts with several CIA officers as well.

Miller said, "You work for Khaled?"

"I used to. I got too old for him. Now it's down to this."

It was always down to this, Miller thought. Not for the first time, Miller felt the cop's sympathy for a hooker. Gina Canale was deluded and spiritually dead like most of them. The eyes hard and calculating. "High-class" ones credited themselves for staying only in five-star hotels and not having to stand on street corners or working casinos. Gina Canale had no doubt seen her share of multimillion-dollar yachts and orgies with Arab princes, but the toll was usually the same.

Miller said, "What did Posner have to do with Khaled?"

"I don't know. He said he had some information that Nizar made some kind of deal with the Americans."

"What sort of deal?"

"Something to do with Syria. He wanted me to confirm it for him or something. Maybe get confirmation from Nizar."

"Where's Nizar now?"

"He's in Switzerland. He's under house arrest. He ain't in no jail." She smiled again.

Miller said, "I read something about that. He was arrested for concealing funds, wasn't he?"

Gina shrugged. "They always after him for something. It never sticks."

"Sometimes it does stick."

"Not on him, man. He ain't no federal agent getting a paycheck. He buys men like you."

"Did he try to buy Posner?"

She shrugged again. "I don't know."

"Tell me what you do know. Tell me what you did."

"I didn't do nothing."

"Did you call Nizar?"

"What?"

Miller got out of his chair and walked over to her. He lifted her chin with his hand.

"Did you call Nizar and tell him about Posner's questions?"

"Now you touch me?" She was looking back at him, but some of the steel had left her jaw.

Miller grabbed her shirt collar and pulled it tight. "Did you?"

"You hit me, I call the police."

"Answer me. Did you tell Nizar about Posner?"

"Yeah."

"And what did Nizar say?"

"He said not to worry about it. He said not to talk to the guy again."

"And then?"

"Then he sent me a check for five thousand dollars."

Miller released her.

"Look man," she said, "I didn't know nothing about him getting killed. I didn't know nothing about that."

Miller sighed. "I believe you." He wished he didn't.

Miller took his coat off the chair.

Gina Canale said, "You not going to pay me?"

Miller said, "I think you've been paid enough."

She called him a couple of names in Italian and English. *Bas-*

tardo, motherfucker, so forth. She spoke quickly in her anger, in the Latin fashion. At the door, Miller turned to her. He was feeling very tired.

"Listen," Miller said. "I'm going to give you some advice that's worth more than money. Do not tell anyone else about this. The people who killed Posner wouldn't hesitate to kill you. Maybe Khaled will protect you because you're an old friend. Maybe he kept your name from them to protect you. But you can only be lucky for so long."

She called him another name and he left.

CHAPTER THIRTY

Anne Posner said, "I think you're trying to be nice."

"Why would you think that?" Miller said.

"Telling me my husband didn't sleep with her. You don't have to do that."

They were in the Jaguar negotiating late-afternoon traffic, a lot of stop and go in Georgetown. Miller recognized a townhouse he had worked security at many years ago. A different time then, and he had been a different man. He found himself nostalgic for that time, envying the younger, more innocent man he used to be. A man bored by Washington, D.C., and not afraid of it.

Miller said, "I'm not doing you any favors. Your husband saw that woman because he was trying to get information from her. I suspect he was working alone, doing what he believed was an independent investigation. I thought maybe he was trying to find evidence of torture, but I was wrong about that. He was looking into something else."

"What?"

"A deal. Some sort of agreement between Khaled and Tanner. . . . No, not Tanner. Probably between Gehlen and Khaled. Tanner is working for Gehlen. I've been focusing too much on Tanner. For reasons of my own."

"You don't think this is connected to you?"

"Not directly. I met with a man who used to work with Tanner. He told me that your husband probably turned up something that was not related to me, but rather to the larger picture. I think now he was right."

"What larger picture?"

"The war in Syria. Khaled has contacts everywhere. His fingers in many pies. He's part Syrian himself. He's in trouble with the law. I think a deal was made between him and Gehlen and maybe Ms. Horvath. He lined them up with a man in Syria to give them what they needed to justify the war. In exchange, he probably wants their help in getting out of this criminal case pending against him in Switzerland. A pardon perhaps. Or some grant of immunity."

"A quid pro quo?"

"Something like that."

"And you were what? A loose end?"

Miller nodded. "Something like that."

"And what about Paul?"

"He was trying to do the right thing, but he should not have taken it on by himself."

"I thought you said you liked my husband."

"He struck me as an honorable man. But as Ms. Canale said, he was naive."

Anne Posner's voice broke as she said, "That's—that's unkind."

"I'm sorry, Anne. I don't mean it to be." Miller turned to her. "I don't."

Anne was crying now. "They put you in prison," she said. "They didn't do that for him. They didn't give him that. I wish I didn't know any of this. I wish I'd gone back to Pittsburgh."

"I wish you had too," Miller said. "But we are here now and we can't undo any of it."

"Why did you come here?"

Miller wondered if she really wanted to know. She was angry at him for bringing this ugliness into her life.

Miller said, "I came here for money. I wanted Horvath and her gang to pay me for what they put me through. But then I met with her and somehow she changed my mind. I'm going to tell you something: I suspected she had your husband killed before I met with Lindsey Horvath and yet I still went to her with the intention of demanding payment. I'm sorry for that, but it is what I did."

"How did she change your mind?"

"I can't say for sure. I suppose the murder of your husband changed things. When I realized that she was behind it, that she was not ashamed or sorry about it, I changed my mind. I couldn't accept money from her even if she had offered it. Not that she did offer it."

"Would you have considered it blood money?"

"What do you think?"

"I think people like her and this Khaled are monsters who buy their way out of everything. I don't think they'll ever answer for what they did to Paul. I think you should have taken the money while you could have."

"I don't think you mean that. In fact, I know you don't. In any event, it was never offered, so the point is moot."

"Well, let me ask you something: if you decided not to take money from them, why did you stay here? Why didn't you go home?"

"Because I want her and Gehlen and Tanner to answer for what they did to me. And him."

"And how the hell are you going to do that? How are you going to make them answer for it? Go to the Department of Justice and tell them you got some sort of evidence from a prostitute in a hotel room?"

"No, that won't work. I reveal her name and they'll only kill her too. I don't want any more victims. Even so, it wouldn't do any good. I am a German citizen who went to prison for selling cocaine. A disgruntled former desk analyst, probably mentally unstable. That's what they'll say. My word won't mean anything."

"What about this Khaled? Would he give evidence?"

Miller smiled and shook his head. "People like Khaled don't give evidence. He's got a thousand deals like this working and he's going to keep them all secret."

"Well, that's great."

"For what it's worth, I don't think Khaled wanted your husband killed. Murder's not his style. He's just a businessman and a playboy and a bit of a pimp. But he's no terrorist."

"Well, my husband's dead. I don't know why you feel the need to defend this man."

"He's dead because Lindsey Horvath had him killed."

Anne Posner looked out at the traffic in front of them. After a few moments, she said, "I don't know what to think of you."

"I'm sorry," Miller said. "About all of it."

"It's not your fault. I don't want a drink right now. Do you believe me?"

"Yes."

"I don't want to be alone either. I don't want to go home right now. Will you take me someplace? Please?"

CHAPTER THIRTY-ONE

Anne washed her face and hands in the sink of Miller's hotel room. She looked in the mirror at her face and then beyond that to a reflection of Miller sitting at the table. A gun was on the table. It was the first time she had seen it.

She turned and said, "Have you had that all along?"

"It was in the car."

"Have you used it?"

"Why do you want to know?"

After a moment, she said, "I guess I don't. You said before you were mentally unstable."

"I said that's what they would say."

"I don't like guns."

"I don't blame you."

She left the sink and walked around the room, restless. After pacing for a bit she sat down on the bed.

Miller looked at her and thought for a moment. He picked up the Ruger pistol and walked over to her. He looked at her briefly. Then he set the gun on the nightstand next to her and walked back to the table and sat down.

Anne Posner smiled and shook her head. "That wasn't necessary. I'm not afraid of you."

"I didn't say you were."

"You were worried that I was. That's why you set the gun next to me. Giving me the illusion of control and comfort."

"I just don't want you to worry."

"I'm not worried about you." She put her fingers on the gun, felt its cold steel. Took her fingers off. "Have you killed people before?"

"It's not your business."

"My husband's been killed. It seems to have become my business."

"I was a soldier a long time ago. Yes, in combat situations, I took some lives. Then I was an analyst, working at a desk. Interviewing suspects, reading reports mostly. I preferred the desk to the field."

"So you're not licensed to kill?"

Miller shook his head, smiling. "The intelligence business generally doesn't work like that."

"You mean it's not supposed to."

"No. It's not supposed to."

"Sorry."

"For what?"

"For asking if you were mentally unstable. I never thought you were."

"That's good to know."

"You Germans, you're kind of a blunt people, aren't you?"

"Rude may be a better word."

"Or frank. No, don't misunderstand me. I'm glad you gave me heat about the drinking, about the self-loathing. You didn't intend to help me, but you did."

"I already told you—"

"I know what you told me. That you said that in anger. But I don't want that lingering between us anymore. I want you to know that I'm not angry about that anymore."

"Okay."

Anne Horvath looked at the gun again and then back at Miller. "You know something, I have an aunt who worked in the publishing business. Aunt Sadie. She worked for this big house in New York editing thrillers. We used to get all these free books from her when I was a kid. My dad read them all and he never threw any of them out. I read some of them myself. It seemed like every month there was a book issued with the premise that a Fourth Reich was going to take over the world."

"We make wonderful bad guys."

"You sure sold a lot of books. You ever read *The Boys From Brazil?*"

"No."

"*Marathon Man?*"

"No. I think I saw the film, though. Was that the one where the Nazi tortures someone with a dentist's drill?"

"Yes. Laurence Olivier. Dustin Hoffman's the good guy. He was supposed to be a college student in the movie, but I think he was around forty at the time."

"He's the little fellow, right?"

"Yeah. Great actor, though. He was a movie star back when movie stars were more interesting-looking than pretty."

"Like your Bogart, uh?"

"You like Humphrey Bogart?"

The German seemed to come alive. "Oh, yes. My favorite when I was a boy. I probably saw *Sahara* ten times."

"Weren't the Germans the bad guys in that movie?"

"Ah, yes. Shooting unarmed people in the back and so forth. In the films, all the Germans were Nazis. They made that film during the war. A morale booster for the Allies. There's a scene when Bogie praises the Russians fighting in Moscow to rouse his men. It's completely out of place, but I suppose the film-makers wanted to include them in the war effort. But still, all in all, a great film. Bogart said it was his favorite, I think."

"It surprises me that you would like it."

"Why? Look, Europeans make a great show of disdaining American culture. But the dirty secret is, we love your movies.

The English, the German, even the French, they grow up watching your Redfords and McQueens and Paul Newmans and they think America must be the greatest place in the world where every man is handsome and every woman is beautiful."

"What about John Wayne?"

"Ah, well, John Wayne . . ."

"Yeah, I know. When a European gets started on John Wayne, look out."

"I think he was actually an underrated actor. But *The Green Berets* was utter silliness."

"I didn't see that one."

"Try not to."

"Did you see *Inglourious Basterds*?"

"Yes, unfortunately."

"You didn't like it?"

"It was interesting. I must say, I don't really quite get your Tarantino. Europeans love him, though."

Anne laughed. She said, "I saw it with Paul. Do you know what he said about it? He said the most interesting characters in the film were the Germans. I think it was supposed to be Brad Pitt's movie, but his character was the dullest in the film."

"I found myself confused by it as well. I even wondered if it was anti-Semitic. The scene where the American Jewish soldier kills the unarmed German because he won't reveal where his *kamerads* are, the German soldier looked courageous while the Jew came off as savage."

"I guess I missed that."

"It was the scene with the baseball bat. Pornographic, in my view. But Germans in general liked the film."

"Really?"

"Yes."

"That's odd, if you don't mind me saying."

"I don't mind. You misunderstand. The generation that fought for Hitler, they're all gone now."

"I don't really understand you." She looked at him for a moment. "I like you, though."

"I like you too."

"Do you mean that?" she said. "You're not so easy to read."

"Yes, I mean it."

She looked at Miller for a while. Miller looked back, uncomfortable in that moment. Then he said, "Listen, I've been thinking about something. I think I should drive you to Pittsburgh tonight. I'd like to do that if you'll let me."

She looked at him some more. "Are you worried about me?"

"A little, yes. I think you would be safer there."

"I'll think about that, Kurt. But if I agree to it, will you promise not to come back to Washington?"

"I don't know if I can promise that."

"Can you at least lie to me and tell me you'll consider it?"

"Yes. I'll consider it."

Anne Posner got off the bed and walked over to Miller. She stood in front of him. Then she moved closer to him and put her hand on his shoulder. Miller took her hand and held it. He turned her hand over and kissed her wrist. Anne bent over and kissed him on the mouth. Then she took him by the hand and led him back to the bed.

CHAPTER THIRTY-TWO

It was dark when Miller drove her back to her house. Anne was quiet in the car. She rested her hand on his neck for a few moments, but that was all. She had agreed to let him drive her back to Pittsburgh after she picked up some things at her home. Miller was afraid she would change her mind if he started talking to her.

She had been passionate, very passionate in bed. They said in the army that it was always the quiet ones, but guys in the army said a lot of things. Miller suspected her passion was connected to grief or maybe even fear. But he knew that he had needed her as much as she needed him. He too was frightened and alone and vulnerable.

When they reached her house, she turned to him and put a hand on his face.

"Thank you."

"For what?" Miller said.

She smiled and leaned over and kissed him lightly on the mouth.

Miller unhitched his seatbelt and kissed her back. He drew away from her. He thought about the drive to Pittsburgh. Maybe they could stay at a hotel along the way. The thought of waking up with her was pleasant. Then he heard the sound of an engine and he turned to look in the rearview mirror. A Chevy Suburban pulling up behind the Jaguar. Miller stiffened and the Suburban hit the back of the Jaguar and pushed it against the garage door, pinning it.

Miller hit his head on the steering wheel. It disoriented him and he looked over to Anne as she cried out. Her seatbelt was still on and that was good. Miller remembered he had put the Ruger in the glove compartment. It would still be there, he thought. But then a burly man yanked his door open and pulled Miller out. The burly man held him tight while another man hit him twice in the head with the butt of a shotgun. After the second hit, Miller slumped to the ground.

CHAPTER THIRTY-THREE

Lyle Waters, the burly man, kicked Miller until he came to.

Miller heard Tanner's voice before he opened his eyes. "Okay, he's coming around. Put him on the chair."

Miller opened his eyes as they put him on a folding chair. His hands were tied fast in front of him with flexicuffs. The same kind the American soldiers used on insurgents in Iraq. They were disposable, unlike regular handcuffs, and they were cheap, but they cut into the skin more.

Miller took in the table and then the rest of his surroundings. He was in the kitchen area of some sort of lake house. The house was run down and may have held some value forty years ago. It was an open-space design, constructed in the seventies. The dining area was next to a kitchen counter and bar. A shabby off-white refrigerator next to the stove. Tanner stood behind the bar. Miller looked into the living room. It was surrounded by large windows looking onto a dark, open body of water. There were no boats on the water.

In the living room were a couch and a couple of chairs. Anne lay on the couch, her hands bound in front of her with flexi-cuffs, her mouth bound by a washcloth. She looked at him with a desperate fear in her eyes. Miller nodded to her, again trying to give her some false comfort. It didn't seem to make her feel any better.

Three men were in the living room. Two of them watching something on television. One of them holding an Uzi submachine gun across his lap. Both of the men watching television were drinking Budweiser from cans. The third man watched Anne Posner. Miller did not like the look on his face.

Lyle Waters took a seat at the table, at a right angle to Miller. His hand was on a Glock pistol, his finger on the trigger. The gun was pointed at Miller.

Tanner said, "How you feeling, boy?"

Miller said, "Like morning after Oktoberfest."

A couple of the men in the living room laughed. Even Lyle smirked. They hadn't expected him to crack wise.

Tanner smiled too. He washed a glass in the sink and then poured some Bud into it. He said, "You got style, *kamerad.* I'll give you that."

"My head is buzzing. Like Sylvester the cat with the stars running round and round."

The men laughed again. Miller hadn't thought it was that funny. He was just trying to hide his fear. Maybe they thought his German accent was humorous.

Tanner said, "Well, this cat's in a lot of trouble. Bet I know what you're thinking now."

"What am I thinking?"

"You're thinking, why haven't they killed me yet?"

"The thought had occurred to me."

"It occurred to the boys too," Tanner said. "If I left it to them, they'd put a bullet in your head and take your corpse out on my fishing boat and dump it in the lake."

"They are anxious to get it done, huh?"

"They're bored."

"It's a soldier's right to complain."

Tanner smiled again. "Sure. But they don't have my foresight. I have to consider the bigger picture."

"Of course."

"Kurt—you don't mind if I call you Kurt?"

Miller shrugged.

"Kurt, I know you think I'm some sort of monster. But you're wrong about me. Like you, I'm a soldier. So I'm going to offer you something that I want you to think about."

"What's that?"

"Well, the bad news is, you're going to die no matter what happens. Sorry, but that's how it is. The good news is, I'm not going to torture you before you die. If you play nice."

"And how do I play nice?"

"Here's the thing: I know you've been snooping around my country asking a lot of stupid questions and getting people upset. You tell me the names of everyone you talked to and I won't torture you. You'll die a quick, painless death. Ms. Posner over there will too. No rape, no cutting off fingers or pulling off toenails. You just tell me what I need to know and it will be easier for everyone."

"Well, I would if I could. But I haven't talked to anyone other than you and Ms. Horvath."

Tanner sighed and looked at Lyle. "See, we're off to a bad start. I know, Kurt, that you're lying. You talked to Bill Carson."

"Yes, but you already knew that. I have not deceived you."

"I'm attempting to have a good-faith discussion here and I'm not getting good faith in return. Lyle?"

Lyle Waters walked over to Miller and punched him in the face. Miller was knocked off his seat.

Anne Posner made a muffled cry behind her gag.

Lyle pulled Miller up by his shirt front and put him back on the chair.

Tanner said, "You see that Lyle likes to hurt people. He's kind of primal. Right, Lyle?"

Lyle grunted.

Tanner said, "I credit you for being able to take a punch. Lyle's got a mean right cross. But if you don't cooperate, it's not just going to be a series of punches that are going to be inflicted on you. It'll be a lot worse than that. And before you start picturing water being poured over your nose and mouth, let me disabuse you of that fantasy. We're not talking about waterboarding. We're talking harsh measures. Eyes gouged out with spoons, hands placed over open flames, that sort of thing. Do you understand me?"

"I understand you very well."

"Good. Now let's clear the air about something. I know you're lying already and not just about Carson. I know for a fact that you talked with Harry Feld. Harry's dead now, so that's taken care of. But what I don't know is, who else you talked to. The guy I work for, Mr. Gehlen, these sort of loose ends make him nervous. And when he gets nervous, he nags me and then I get upset."

"Gehlen ordered this?"

"Yeah. I have to go into Frederick and bring him back. That way, he'll be here when you spill—and you will—and then I won't have to listen to him nag anymore." Tanner looked at his watch. "So that gives you about a half hour to think about what we talked about. And I want you to think about it, Kurt. You're a German and I'm an American. We're both products of western civilization. And I'm offering you a civilized alternative here."

"May I have a drink while I'm thinking?" Miller smiled. "From one civilized man to another."

Tanner laughed. "Well, at least you got some sense. Can you stomach our American beer?"

It struck Miller as funny, that. It was the second time an American had asked him that question. Miller said, "Better than nothing."

Tanner said, "We'll give you some in a plastic cup. Wouldn't want you breaking a glass and using it on any of these mothers' necks."

Tanner snapped his fingers at one of the men in the living room. The man looked at him and Tanner pointed to the dining room table. The man, whose name was Carter, came over and took a place at the table opposite Lyle. Carter held the shotgun he had hit Miller with earlier. Now Miller was guarded by armed men on both sides. The barrel of Lyle's pistol still aimed at his midsection.

"Keep him alive until I get back," Tanner said. "Unless he tries something, then kill him."

"He's not going anywhere," Lyle said. Looking at Miller as he said it.

"Make sure he doesn't," Tanner said.

Tanner drove the black Mercedes down the narrow winding road past a number of unlit lake homes. The place used to be something years ago. The lake house had belonged to the family of his first wife. They had used it all the time when she was growing up. His first wife thought it was something special. Tanner thought it was a dump. He had taken it in the divorce settlement, though. His wife had gotten too good for it, had outgrown it. Tanner had thought back then he could level the house and sell the property, but then he had changed his mind and held onto it. He had found other uses for it. It was isolated and conveniently located. About a ninety-minute drive from Washington.

Back at the Posner house, Carter had wanted to keep beating on the German's head with the shotgun until it split like a melon. It was Tanner who had stopped him. Tanner had said, "We need him alive for now." That was all he said. He had learned over the years not to tell his people everything he was thinking.

He would not tell Carter or Lyle why he wanted the German alive for now. The truth was, it was something the German himself had said to him. When they were in New York, it was the German who had told Tanner that Gehlen and Lindsey Horvath would sell him out when the heat came down. Tanner dismissed it at first—just some shit the German had said to rattle him. But over the next few days, he thought about it and realized there was something to it. If things ever broke, if the FBI or some sort of Senate investigative committee ever came knocking, Gehlen was just the sort to give him up. *I had no idea that would happen,* Gehlen would say. Or, *I never authorized that.* Some such shit.

It had pleased Tanner when Gehlen came out to meet him when Tanner and his men were target shooting. Gehlen was uncomfortable, maybe even scared, and trying his best not to show it. Gehlen obviously looked down on Tanner's men. Rough, dangerous types. *Vulgar* would probably be the word Gehlen would use to describe them. Bad-asses who kept little men like Gehlen protected.

Well, they *were* bad-asses. Tattooed, hard, squinty-eyed men who would have probably been in prison if Tanner or some other agency man hadn't corralled them into service. But what did Gehlen expect? Men who protected our freedoms could not be expected to come out of Groton or Exeter or whatever faggoty place it was that bred men like Jay Gehlen.

Tanner wanted to bring Gehlen a little closer to the fire. Not to kill him; Tanner needed him too much for that. And maybe not even to scare Gehlen, though that thought had occurred to Tanner too. No, the main thing he wanted was to have Gehlen there when they tortured the German and killed him and dumped his body in the lake. He wanted Gehlen there for all of it. That way, Gehlen would be part of it, his hands as dirty as everyone else's. A co-conspirator. A murderer. After that, Gehlen wouldn't be able to offer him up to anyone because he would be in it himself. Up to his neck.

CHAPTER THIRTY-FOUR

Miller drank three cups of beer. It was watery, shitty stuff. Three-point-two content American shit. As a young man, Miller had done his share of Bavarian beerfests. All the stereotypes of Germans had been in abundance: plates of sausages, fat drunk men in lederhosen, soused sweaty krauts singing along in perfect unison with some asshole on a stage, people passed out under tables. A gross part of their heritage that no amount of Allied bombs could ever extinguish.

But Mother of God, Germans could drink.

Even Miller.

He pushed the empty cup back to Lyle Waters.

"More?" Lyle said.

"Bitte."

"Beat-ah?"

Carter said, "It's German for please, dumbass."

It seemed to amuse them when he spoke German. It showed them that he was drunk and merry and maybe a bit of a clown. Miller considered what he looked like to them. An undersized man with a black eye that Lyle had given him and a big knotty bruise that Carter had put on his head. Getting drunk because he was scared or crazy or maybe just a fool. They were not afraid of him. And that was something.

Carter went to the refrigerator and brought back two more cans of beer. Popped one open and refilled Miller's red plastic cup.

Miller held the red cup up.

"*Prost.*"

"Cheers to you, kraut," Carter said. He sat down at the table and put the shotgun on top of it. The barrel pointed at Miller's chest, Carter's finger on the trigger.

Miller emptied his cup in two gulps.

"Another," Miller said.

Lyle said, "You're hitting that shit pretty hard."

"*Ach so.* I plan to get very drunk."

"You'll still feel pain, when the time comes," Lyle said.

"But not as much."

Lyle gestured with his head to the lake outside. "Water's cold out there. Not cold enough to ice over, but pretty fucking cold. But you won't feel it when we put you in it."

Miller looked at him, his eyes glazing. "Are we going swimming?"

Carter laughed at that one. And even Lyle smiled.

Anne screamed. Miller turned to look, keeping his expression bleary. The tall man who had been leering at her had taken the gag out of her mouth. He was trying to kiss her now. Anne turning her head away from him. The man had left his handgun on the table by the television. Apparently so that Anne couldn't take it out of his belt and use it on him. The man who held the Uzi on his lap was laughing. They had both been drinking.

"Goddammit, Jett," Lyle said. "Can't you wait until later?"

The man named Jett was holding Anne by the neck now, keeping her head steady as he put his mouth on hers. His other hand now up her shirt.

Lyle turned back to see the German smiling drunkenly at him.

"The *fraulein* is attractive, uh? A nice little piece of hide, uh?"

Carter laughed at the little German. "How would you know?"

"How would I know!" Miller was loud and his voice a little

more German than normal. They seemed to like that. "You asking me how I know?"

"Yeah."

Miller gestured with his head, like he was getting ready to confide something to them. Carter moved closer. Miller looked around as if to see if anyone else could eavesdrop.

Miller said, "I'll tell you something, friend. I had her up. I had her down." Miller rolled his head. "And I had her all the way around."

Carter barked out a laugh. "Goddammit, you crack me up."

"Don't laugh at me. I am serious."

"Yeah, well, I think you're full of shit."

"You don't believe me?"

"No," Carter said. But he was looking past Miller now. Looking at Anne as she sat back on the couch crying. Jett standing away from her as he took a break, laughing and saying, "Just relax, darling. Don't you want to relax?"

Miller said, "You don't?"

Carter was surprised to find the kraut still staring at him. Like he was offended or something. Carter said, "Don't what?"

"You don't believe me?"

Carter said, "No, partner, I don't."

"Let me tell you something, *partner*. You know what she has on her pelvis, next to her lovely little *muschi*?"

"What?"

And now even Lyle was watching him with interest. And the men in the living room were interested too. Jett moving a few steps closer to them, the short man with the Uzi getting to his feet. Miller had their attention.

Miller said, "A tattoo."

"Fuck," Lyle said, smirking.

"Shit," Carter said, "this is the twenty-first century. *Grandmas* got tattoos these days."

"No, no," Miller said. "Not like this one. This one is special."

"Let me guess," Carter said, "A rose petal. Or, what, a Chinese dragon?"

"No, much better than that. You ever watch football?"

"Yeah. So what?"

"She's got a tattoo of the logo for the Pittsburgh Steelers."

Now Carter and the two men in the living room were whooping with laughter. Anne sitting up, something like a look of horror spreading on her face.

"I've seen it," Miller said. "I tell you, man, I've seen it. I've never been so pleasantly surprised in my life."

"Bullshit."

"You are calling me a liar?"

"Yeah," Carter said, still amused.

Miller said, "Well, why don't you see for yourself?"

The smile spread against Carter's face. He downed his beer and said, "I believe I will."

Carter left, taking his shotgun with him. Lyle stayed at the table. Miller kept smiling. And then Anne was screaming again as she came off the couch as the men approached her. She tried to run around the couch as Jett chased her, and then the short man put his Uzi on his chair and went around to the other side of the couch to cut her off. Carter put his shotgun on top of the high shelf over the television and joined the other two. Anne jumped over the back of the couch and then stumbled as the men closed on her. She struggled and screamed and they put her on the floor. Jett held her down by the shoulders and the short man pinned her hands at her sides. Carter began to unbutton her pants.

The moment came when Lyle had to turn and watch. When he turned he took his Glock pistol with him, holding it in front of his chest and stomach. Miller would have preferred that he left the pistol on the table, but he would take what he could get.

Lyle said, "Just pull 'em off by the cuffs, you fuckin' ya-hooes!"

Silently, Miller leapt on Lyle and threw his arms over his neck and grabbed his pistol. Lyle didn't have time to struggle until the pistol was turned and lifted in front of his chest, but by then he was too late, as Miller had the momentum and Miller kept pulling and turning the pistol up until the barrel was under Lyle's chin and Miller pulled the trigger.

An explosion of blood and brain, some of which splattered onto Miller's face. Carter looking up from Anne Posner's naked thighs as Miller leveled the Glock and shot Carter twice in the chest. Then it was Jett who stood up and Miller shot him twice in the chest and once in the head.

The short man moved quickly, running away from Anne to the Uzi he had left on the chair. He reached it just as Miller shot him twice in the back.

The short man was on his stomach and still breathing. Miller walked up to him and shot him in the back of the head and the breathing ended. Then he walked over to Carter and did the same. Just to be sure.

Anne Posner pulling up her jeans now, over her panties. Her mouth was open and she started to turn to the corpse of Lyle Waters, to see where it all began, and Miller stopped her.

"Don't!" Miller said. "Don't look at any of them. Go to the kitchen and get a knife that can cut through these things. Hurry now."

She stood up and buttoned her pants. Looking now at the German with the bits of blood and God knew what else on his face and neck. This apparition she had politely shared a bed with only a few hours ago. She began to waver.

"Anne! Not now. It's a horrible thing you've seen, but we're alive and they're dead. You want to stay alive, do as I say. Please."

CHAPTER THIRTY-FIVE

Miller found the Jaguar outside the lake house. Anne told him they had brought it here with them. She told him they had put her in the trunk. She said they had put him in the trunk of the Mercedes; the one Tanner was driving. She told him these things as he patiently asked her what had happened while he was unconscious.

Miller checked the glove compartment of the Jaguar. The Ruger was still in there. Miller took the Ruger out of the glove compartment and checked the rounds. He put the loaded Ruger under the front seat. Then he picked the Uzi submachine gun off the hood of the car. He still had the Glock pistol in his coat pocket.

Anne said, "We haven't much time. Tanner said he would be back soon."

"I know that." Miller went to the trunk of the Jaguar and opened it. He lifted the lid over the spare tire and took a cellular phone out of a box. He clicked the phone on and put it in his pocket.

"Kurt, come *on*. Let's go."

"Anne, listen to me. I need you to do something. I need you to stay here with me."

"What?"

"If we go, they'll find us. If not tomorrow, soon after. I have to finish this."

"But—"

"If we leave here now, they'll notice the car is gone and then we lose our advantage. They have to still think we're captive. They have to think we're still in there."

"Kurt—"

"*Listen to me.* I need them in the house. Guns aren't much use in the dark. I need them in the house."

She looked at him again, thinking about the man who she had been intimate with and the man who had killed four men in the space of a few seconds. The same man.

Anne said, "I can't go back in there. Please don't ask me to go back in there."

"I won't." Miller pointed to the darkened home across the drive. "Hide over there until they come. After they've gone in, count to sixty and then get in the car and go. Don't stop for anyone or anything until you get to Frederick. Park the car where it can't be seen from the road. If I don't call you within one hour, go. Drive to Pittsburgh. Do not go back to Washington. I left the gun under the seat. If someone stops you that's not a policeman, kill him and keep moving."

"You can't go back in there, Kurt. Tanner said he was going to kill you."

"He said a lot of things; he's a talker." Miller looked back to the house with a determined expression Anne Posner had never seen before. "Now I'm going to say something to him."

My God, Anne thought. He's a killer himself. Maybe born and maybe made, but one all the same. He hadn't just been lucky in that house. He had used her to distract them and then he had killed them. He hadn't hesitated at all. He had planned it and he had done it. God knew what cold history was in the file of his life. And though deep down, she knew there had been no other way—no realistic alternative to demand the men put up their hands and surrender—she realized that he could well be a man she wouldn't want to know in a few weeks and maybe not even want to know tomorrow. But . . . tomorrow seemed like a very long time from now. And right now she was very glad to have him on her side.

She said, "I don't want to leave you."

"You won't be."

She hesitated for a moment, wondering if she should say something else.

Miller said, "Go now. Everything will be all right." Some of the kindness back in his tone now and Anne Posner was grateful to have that part of him back.

Miller waited until she crouched behind a trash dumpster.

Then he went into the house. He picked up the shotgun and Jett's pistol and went out on the back deck and hurled them into the lake. He heard the satisfying sound of the consecutive splashes and went back inside. He turned the television back on and turned up the volume very loud. A college football game with a lot of roars.

Then he started to move the bodies.

The high-beam lights of the Mercedes illuminated the Chevy Suburban and the Jaguar. Tanner parked the Mercedes in the sally port to the left of the house. Gehlen got out of the passenger side. Gehlen was in his off-duty clothes: slacks, oxford shirt, and pullover sweater. Parka over that.

Gehlen said, "You've got the woman too?"

Tanner said, "I already told you we did."

Gehlen nodded. "Well, it's her fault for trying to help him."

Gehlen accepted the fact that they would have to kill her too. He was still conventional enough in his thinking though to hope that Tanner's men hadn't raped her. It was unfortunate that white women had to be part of such things, but she should have stayed out of it.

Tanner said, "Miller might have talked already. Maybe to

keep them from harming the woman."

"If he has, he'll have to do it again."

Tanner sighed in the dark. Gehlen trying to talk tough again. Trying to let Tanner know it was his show at the end of the day.

Gehlen followed Tanner through the front door. Right away, they heard the television blaring. They walked through the front corridor and came out into the living room area.

And saw no one.

Tanner said, "What the fuck?"

Tanner took his pistol out of his coat and proceeded forward, Gehlen following. And then Tanner was past the kitchen counter and bar. He looked at the dining room table and saw that no one was sitting on it.

Then he saw the bodies of the four men on the floor on the other side of the table.

"Jesus Christ!"

His four men piled on the floor. All of them dead, Lyle with his face blown off.

Gehlen standing next to him now. Seeing what Tanner was seeing and right away he started to shake.

"Tanner," Miller said. "Drop the gun on the floor."

Tanner turned to see Miller holding the Uzi on him. Tanner's pistol still at his side, but the German had the barrel of the machine gun pointed right at him, his finger on the trigger.

Now it was Gehlen saying, "Christ."

Miller kept his eyes on Tanner and said, "We can talk or you can die. It's up to you."

Tanner let his pistol drop to the floor. He straightened up and put the fear out of his expression. Then he smiled.

"What happened?" Tanner said.

"They got careless."

"I see that," Tanner said. "It happens when you let men drink on duty."

"It happens when you hire the wrong men."

"There are more where that came from," Tanner said.

Miller said, "But not here."

Tanner smiled again. "Okay, Kurt. You got us. Now what? You going to kill us too?"

Outside the Jaguar's engine turned over. The three men listened as the car moved into gear and drove away.

"Goddammit," Tanner said.

"Who is that?" Gehlen said.

Tanner said, "It's the woman, Jay. Miller left the car there so we would be tricked into coming into the house."

"Oh, shit," Gehlen said. "She's going to come back here with the cops."

"No, you needn't worry about that," Miller said. "No policemen, Mr. Gehlen. Just a few men having a friendly chat."

"Yeah," Tanner said. "He doesn't want the cops here. He's here to collect his money. Two million now, right? Well, we don't have anything like that here. So what are we going to do?"

Miller frowned. He looked at Tanner and then at Gehlen.

"Two million?" Miller said. "Where did you get that from?"

Gehlen said, "That's what Lindsey told us."

"Really?" Miller looked at Gehlen. "Is that what she told you?"

"Yeah," Gehlen said.

"Then she was lying," Miller said. "I told her I don't want the money anymore. Any of it."

Gehlen said, "But she told me—"

"She lied to you, Mr. Gehlen. Probably not for the first time. You people lie to each other so much, I don't know how you get along. Yes, I spoke with Ms. Horvath and when I realized she had had Posner killed, I decided I wanted no part of her or her money."

Tanner said, "Then what are you still doing in the States?"

"I stayed here because I wanted to prove the three of you conspired to murder Posner."

"Well then you've wasted your time," Tanner said. "You're not going to be able to prove anything." Tanner gestured with his head to the corpses. "Consider the situation: you just killed four American citizens. Including Hayes, that makes five. Go to the FBI, go to the Justice Department. Who do you think they're going to arrest?"

"Maybe all of us," Miller said. "You can tell them your story and I'll tell them mine."

Gehlen said, "Look, I had nothing to do with Posner. That was Tanner's doing."

Tanner turned to look at Gehlen.

"Jay."

Gehlen looked at Tanner and then back at Miller. "I'm serious. I didn't authorize that."

"Jay," Tanner said, "you ordered it. You and Lindsey both."

"I only said—"

"I know what you said," Tanner said. "I was there. What's the point of lying about it here?"

Miller looked at Tanner and said, "I told you."

And Tanner thought, yeah, you told me. Gehlen would sell him out. He just didn't think it would be so soon.

And now Gehlen was looking directly at the German, imploring him to take what he said at face value, Gehlen saying, "What I said to Carl was—"

Tanner grabbed Gehlen by his parka and hurled him toward Miller. Gehlen stumbled forward and for a moment he was between Miller and Tanner. Tanner crouched down and reached for his pistol. Miller saw it and moved to the left of Gehlen, one step, then two, and then Gehlen was no longer in his way. Tanner had the pistol in his hand and was lifting it and pointing it and Miller let a burst go from the Uzi. The rounds hit Tanner in his chest and neck and face and Tanner was knocked backward.

Miller hurried over to Tanner to check to see if he was still alive. That was when Jay Gehlen ran between the counter and the refrigerator.

Tanner was dead.

Miller turned to see Gehlen run out the corridor on the right side of the kitchen. Gehlen ran down the hallway to the bedrooms. He got to a door on the side of the house and ran out of it.

Miller went after him. By the time he got outside, Gehlen was running down a hill to the shore of the lake. Miller followed, the Uzi by his side.

CHAPTER THIRTY-SIX

It was dark, not much moonlight, but Miller could see Gehlen now running along a path next to the shore. Gehlen kept running and Miller ran after him. Miller thinking, you could cut him down now, even in this light, but the man was unarmed.

Gehlen got to a dock with three boats in the slips, all of them on platforms, elevated out of the water for the winter. Gehlen ran down the end of the dock and stopped. He looked down and then out at the bleak water and then at the boats that were of no use to him. There was no place he could go but the water.

Miller stopped running when he got about twenty feet from him. Miller slowed to a walk and stopped a few feet from Gehlen.

Gehlen looked at the German and then back at the lake. Then back at Miller. Miller still holding the Uzi.

Miller said, "Well, here we are. Can you swim?"

Gehlen didn't say anything for a while. He looked around the area but didn't see a soul. No lights on in any house except the one he had just run away from. No lights on the other side of the lake, which looked to be almost a mile away.

Gehlen said, "I know how to swim."

"It's about thirty degrees Fahrenheit," Miller said. "But who knows? Maybe the water is warmer."

Gehlen looked back at the lake and then again at Miller.

Miller said, "You are a fan of this waterboarding, uh? Men like you say it is no big thing to torture. Jump in and try to swim to the other side. See how you like it."

"You'll shoot me if I jump in."

"I won't have to shoot you. You'll cramp up and die in a few minutes. Like the people on the *Titanic*. But I could be wrong. You seem to have more than your share of reptilian blood."

Gehlen turned toward Miller, getting some of his back up. "We're not savages, Miller. We didn't stick our enemies in pools of ice-cold water and take scientific notes while they froze to death."

"Ah. You mean like the Nazis?"

"Yeah."

"And I am a Nazi?"

"You're a German."

"Close enough for you, uh? It's easier when you can persuade yourself that your enemies are less than human, isn't it? But let's talk about the present for a moment. You put me in prison, Mr. Gehlen. Why did you do that?"

"You know why already."

"I want to hear it from you."

"You were in the way. We tried to reason with you. But you wouldn't listen."

"I wouldn't protect your precious Eightball?"

"If we hadn't used him, we'd have used somebody else. It was going to happen one way or another."

"Did Khaled set Eightball up for you?"

Gehlen stared at Miller for a few moments, wondering how this man knew so much.

Gehlen said, "Yeah, Khaled helped."

"And what did you promise him in exchange?"

Gehlen shrugged. "To get him out of a jail sentence in Switzerland. Once Lindsey took office. But I think you knew that already."

"I suspected. And now you've confirmed it. And Posner?"

247

"Posner found out about it. We don't know how, but he did. He called me and threatened to go to the Senate Intelligence Committee with it."

"He tried to blackmail you?"

Gehlen laughed. His confidence was back now. He had seen Miller kill Tanner, had seen the evidence that he killed other men. But those men were armed. Gehlen was confident now, confident in his ability to read people, confident that this man would not kill him.

Gehlen said, "No, Paul was too stupid for that. He was your typical Boy Scout. He didn't want the war in Syria. He thought we should *negotiate,* the putz. He was so clueless he thought he could use that Eightball crap to get us to back down on the war. He had no idea, once it starts, you can't stop it. You can't *un*declare a war just because some jerkoff comes along and tells you it was all based on a mistake of fact. People don't care what the truth is."

"People like you don't care."

"Yeah, people like me. And what about people like you, Miller? You know better? Men like me want to protect freedom. We want to protect democracy. To you, it's just a joke. There's a war out there, whether you want to admit it or not. Islamic terrorists want to destroy freedom. They're chopping people's heads off while you whine about pouring water on their faces. Well, I for one am not going to sit back and just watch it happen."

"I've seen terrorism myself, Gehlen. Closer than you have, I believe. I've seen the victims and I've seen the perpetrators. The people who drove those planes into your Towers, a lot of them operated out of Hamburg. One of them took flight lessons in America. Not one of the terrorists on those planes came from Iraq or Afghanistan. They were all from countries allied to your own. Egypt, Jordan, Saudi Arabia. When do you start bombing them?"

"You're oversimplifying it."

"Am I? What about the bombing of those buses in London? Over fifty people murdered that summer. That was done by British Muslims. British *citizens.* How did occupying Iraq and Afghanistan prevent that? At your own Fort Hood, in Texas, an American-born Muslim killed thirteen people. How does putting tanks in Syria prevent that? This sort of threat is a *movement,* Gehlen. It's not resolved by invading and occupying countries. If it were, you'd have to invade Pakistan, Saudi Arabia, London, and Texas after that. Don't you see that you're the one who's oversimplified it? That people like you have made it worse?"

"We have to address the threat."

"I agree with you about that. But you're not addressing it, you're exploiting it. What has happened to Syria since you got your war? The Islamic State has gained control of it and they're killing your soldiers at a rate of thirty a day. You love war so much you ended up *helping* the terrorists. Aided and abetted them so you could enforce your vision of security."

"Don't you speak to me of American soldiers. They're dying for a good cause."

"Your cause. Yours and Ms. Horvath's. And what about Paul Posner? Did he die for that cause too?"

"He died because he wouldn't keep his mouth shut. Sacrifices have to be made."

Miller shook his head. *Sacrifices have to be made.* It was the same thing Lindsey Horvath had said. These people spent too much time with each other.

Miller said, "So you had Tanner kill him."

"Yeah," Gehlen said. "And I'd do it again."

Miller wearily shook his head. He had planned to smile when

he got this admission, but somehow couldn't bring himself to do it.

"I'm sure you would," Miller said quietly.

Miller took a cellular phone out of his coat pocket. He held it up so Gehlen could see it.

"I bought this a couple of days ago," Miller said. "At one of your . . . Targets?"

Gehlen looked at the phone, nodded slowly. For some reason, the thought of this German shopping at Target mystified him.

"Wonderful little thing," Miller said. "They come with recording devices these days. It costs about forty dollars."

Gehlen opened his mouth and closed it.

"I . . ."

"Yes?"

Gehlen said, "I . . . we . . . we can pay you. Two million dollars."

"For this recording?"

"Yeah. I can get it to you in two days. No more of this rough stuff, I promise. You have my word on it."

"Your word." Miller shook his head, disgusted. "I'm afraid it's a little late for that." Miller lowered his weapon. "Good night, Mr. Gehlen."

Miller threw the Uzi into the lake and turned around and started walking back to the shore.

Gehlen watched him walking away. He hoped the German had been bluffing about the tape recording. But he knew he probably hadn't. The German had been too sure of himself. He had even thrown the machine gun into the water. Gehlen looked at the dark waters of the lake. If he jumped in, could he find the machine gun? No, that was out of the question. The German was walking away now and if he had tape, Gehlen would go to prison. It was that simple. Tape equaled prison. The German further away now and Gehlen saw it then, saw it on the dock that ran alongside the slip next to an elevated sailboat.

It was a piece of iron. A spare belaying pin sitting free and easy next to the slip. Gehlen thought of jail and freedom from disgrace and scandal and he hurried over and picked the belaying pin up. It was a good iron weight and Gehlen took it and ran after the German and he didn't care if the German would hear him coming because the German was unarmed now, the German had thrown the machine gun into the water, making some sort of stupid gesture, and now Gehlen could beat him to death and take his phone away from him, and he was closing in on the German now and he saw the German turn in the darkness, the German stopping and reaching into his coat pocket and Gehlen was close and the German said, "Don't! *Don't!*" And Gehlen ran harder to close the gap, the belaying pin raised and the German steadied the Glock at him and fired once, then twice more.

All three of the shots hit Gehlen and he stumbled and fell on the pier, the belaying pin dropping from his grip. Gehlen stood up and teetered toward a boat, reaching out to grab it for support, but he misjudged the distance and fell into the gap between the boat and the dock. He hit the water head first.

The water *was* cold, he thought. Shockingly cold. But he didn't feel it for long.

CHAPTER THIRTY-SEVEN

It was about a month later when Anne Posner heard the story on NPR. She was driving to her sister's house in Pittsburgh. The NPR reporter said that Lindsey Horvath had officially withdrawn her name as a candidate for the presidency. The reporter said that Horvath had been implicated in the scandal where five men had been killed at a cabin north of Washington. State police and the FBI said that Carl Tanner, retired CIA agent and security consultant, had murdered the five men, including former Under Secretary of State Jay Gehlen.

Anne pulled the car over to hear the rest of it. Her hands were shaking.

She said aloud, "It wasn't a cabin."

She was glad she was alone and no one had heard her say it. People might think she was losing her sanity.

The reporter continued:

> *"The murders were linked to Horvath after the German news magazine Der Spiegel printed a story last week asserting that Gehlen and Tanner conspired to murder an analyst working for the Defense Intelligence Agency. Der Spiegel reported that Horvath was aware of the conspiracy."*

Anne thought back to the lake house. Driving Kurt's Jaguar to town and shaking with fear as she kept checking the time. Kurt called her five minutes before she drove away. She wept with relief when he told her he was okay and that he would be with her soon. She kept weeping until he arrived twenty minutes later.

A few hours later, they stopped at a motel in Bedford. There he told her what he thought she needed to know. She remembered him telling her that he had put the pistol he had used in Tanner's hand. He told her that should take care of it.

He told her that there would come a time when she would want to tell someone what happened. That she would want to confess even though she hadn't done anything wrong because the need to confess was very human, but that she would have to resist that impulse for the rest of her life. He told her he was sorry, but there was no other way.

He told her that after he dropped her off in Pittsburgh, they would never see each other again. He said he didn't know if that was what she had wanted, that he wouldn't blame her if that *was* what she wanted, but either way that was how it would have to be. She started to cry again and he said he hoped she didn't think he was a monster.

Anne had said, "I don't think that. I never will."

They made love for the last time in the Bedford motel room and in the morning she asked him to let her know that he was okay when he got back to Germany. He told her he would try.

She got a postcard from him a week ago. He wrote that he was working as a hotel desk clerk in Hamburg and that he liked it more than he thought he would. Anne cried when she read the postcard. Then she burned it.

The radio reporter said:

"The FBI and the Department of Justice are presently investigating Horvath, but have not yet made a determination if criminal charges will be filed. Horvath's attorney said they look forward to examining all the facts and clearing her name."

ABOUT THE AUTHOR

James Patrick Hunt is the author of *Maitland, Maitland Under Siege, Maitland's Reply, Get Maitland, The Betrayers, Goodbye Sister Disco, The Assailant, The Silent Places, Bullet Beth, Reinhardt's Mark, Bridger, Police and Thieves, The Detective,* and *The Reckoning.* He lives in Tulsa, Oklahoma, where he writes and practices law.